CUDDLES MCGEE MAY HAVE
HAMSTER WHEEL IN THE SKY, BUT THAT DOESN'T
MEAN HIS TROUBLEMAKING DAYS ARE OVER.

AND ARLIE, TY, AND MR. BOOTS
ARE JUST ABOUT TO DISCOVER THIS IN:

THE
CURSE
OF
CUDDLES
McGEE

ALSO AVAILABLE FROM EMILY ECTON:

Boots and Pieces

THE CURSE OF CUDDLES McGEE

By Emily Ecton

ALADDIN PAPERBACKS
NEW YORK   LONDON   TORONTO   SYDNEY

To my sister, Sarah.
You rulio, Iglesias!

❧ ALADDIN PAPERBACKS

An imprint of Simon & Schuster Children's Publishing Division

1230 Avenue of the Americas, New York, NY 10020

Text copyright © 2008 by Emily Ecton

Cover illustration © 2008 by Scott M. Fischer

All rights reserved, including the right of reproduction in whole or in part in any form.

ALADDIN PAPERBACKS and related logo are registered trademarks of Simon & Schuster, Inc.

Designed by Lisa Vega

The text of this book was set in Bembo.

Manufactured in the United States of America

First Aladdin Paperbacks edition September 2008

10 9 8 7 6 5 4 3 2 1

Library of Congress Control Number 2008924918

ISBN-13: 978-1-4169-6450-6

ISBN-10: 1-4169-6450-9

CHAPTER 1

I BLAME MR. BOOTS. SURE, I ACCEPT RESPONSI-bility for my actions—I'm not saying I don't. All I'm saying is that none of this would've happened if Mr. Boots hadn't gone around flaunting his privates so much.

Mr. Boots is our dog—basically a mutant Chihuahua—and up until a couple of months ago he was a regular fashion plate. My mom and my sister, Tina, kept him decked out in doggie fashions that had the double advantage of making him a style icon while keeping him decent, if you know what I mean.

I don't want to get into the whole thing here, but a couple of months ago Mr. Boots got into a little trouble, and Tina blamed the outfit. We all decided that it would be best if he just went au naturel for a while. It seemed like a good idea at the time, and Mr. Boots was all for it. And that was the problem.

Let me say right here that I, Arlene Jacobs, have no problem with canine nudity. I've seen other dogs go around in the buff and it's fine, they look perfectly normal. But for some reason, Mr. Boots always looks like he's posing for his *Playdog* pictorial. It's pretty disconcerting. I've learned to avert my eyes, but Mom, well, she's not handling it quite so well. Let me put it this way—we never used to have to stock smelling salts. (Mom likes to call them her personal aromatherapy crystals, but come on, we know what we're talking about here.)

We thought things would get better after a while— you know, Mr. Boots would start acting a little less pervy and Mom would get used to him—but it just wasn't happening. Not to mention the fact that his wardrobe malfunction of a couple of months ago made him a kind of a minor celebrity in our town, resulting in a "Boots Watch" column in the local tabloid and occasional gawkers on the lawn.

So in the middle of dinner last week, Dad had announced that he and Mom were heading out to a spa for a weeklong seaweed wrappapalooza. He said it was because they had mucky pores or something, but everybody knew it was just so Mom could get away from Nudieboots for a while.

So if it hadn't been for Mr. Boots, me and my best friend Ty wouldn't have been killing time at the construction site of the new town pool. But when your dad hands you a naked dog and banishes you from the house so your mother can pack, your options are pretty limited. The construction site was Ty's idea, and I was all for it. I figured, how bad can it be? I mean, bulldozers—that's pretty exciting, right?

Actually, bulldozers are not so exciting when all

3

they're doing is sitting there parked. Apparently bull-dozing is not a 24/7 activity, and we'd missed the actual 'dozing for the day. So instead of an afternoon of wacky bulldozer hijinks, we ended up with a field of churned-up red clay and a couple of hibernating bulldozers. Which is exciting for about thirty seconds, I'd say.

Mr. Boots immediately began a thorough inspection of the area, and me and Ty made the best of it. But honestly, there are only so many ways you can rearrange little flags and only so many times you can pretend you're getting run over by huge bulldozer wheels.

"Arrrghh, Arlie, the pain! I'm totally squished." Ty writhed in front of the bulldozer. Ha-ha, right? Maybe the first time, but I'm serious here, ten times is way too many. It's not even like he looked squished.

"Arrrrghhhhh . . . can't move my legs!" Ty gurgled.

"Getting old, Ty," I said as a big blop of water hit me on the forehead. I peered up at the sky and groaned. Nothing like threatening storm clouds and minor drizzle action to make my day even better.

I squatted down on a clump of clay and tickled Mr. Boots's foot. After his inspection had turned up nothing unusual, Mr. Boots had passed out in a tire track. His face was crusted with red muck and he looked pathetic, but what was even more pathetic was that he looked really comfortable. I tickled his foot again, and he kicked the crap out of my hand without even opening his eyes.

"Agony! I'm in agony, Arlie! Arlie? Aw, crud." Ty finally stopped writhing and got up, shooting me a disgusted look. "Well, fine then." He tried to brush the clay off his pants, but really just succeeded in smearing it around. "Got any better ideas?" He kicked at a big chunk of dirt, spraying me and Mr. Boots with a fine layer of grit. Pretty inconsiderate, if you ask me. And I wasn't thinking of myself—I was thinking of poor Mr. Boots buried nose deep in a shallow tire track grave.

Ty grinned at me. "You see that? Check out this shot." He kicked at another clump of dirt.

"That was awesome, thanks." I spit grit out of my mouth. Seriously, if Mom and Dad wanted mud baths, they should've just come here. "Let's head back. Dad won't care. Especially if it's raining."

"Sounds like a plan," Ty said, doing some fancy soccer footwork and batting at a chunk that promptly disintegrated. "Check this out, though."

I groaned and looked around. There were way too many big chunks of dirt lying around. I should've brought protective eyewear. Ty's decided that he's going to be the next big soccer star, so his big thing this summer has been kicking everything that isn't nailed down. He calls it "training." Beats me if he's any good, but I bet Coach Miller'll go for it, no problem.

Another blop of water landed on my arm. Definitely starting to rain. Mr. Boots was examining a piece of yellow paper, so I waited until it passed inspection and then scooped Mr. Boots up (the element of surprise seems to be the key when he's in a bad mood). I grabbed the paper, too—it looked like it was some kind of flyer. I figured it was probably just some kind of car wash ad, but it would double as a dog wash device in a pinch.

I smoothed out the piece of crumpled paper while Mr. Boots hissed at me. That dog needs to go to anger management classes.

"Hey, Ty, check this out."

Ty had gone into some weird tai chi pose, and I guess I must've startled him, because he kind of toppled to the side in a dorky way.

"Geez, Arlie, ruin my concentration, why don't you?" Ty wiped his mouth and started eyeballing the clump again.

"Forget it." Sure, I was being sulky. According to the paper, the TV show *America's Most Talented Pets* was having auditions at the movie theater this week. An actual, real-life TV show. Big news, okay? But if Ty thought his dirt clump was more important, he could just hear about it later. I stuffed the flyer in my pocket.

Ty had gotten back into his tai chi pose, pointed at a tree at the edge of the lot, and then kicked the heck out of the clump. Except this clump didn't just disintegrate. This clump clanged.

"What the heck?" Dirt clumps don't clang. I jumped up, jostling Mr. Boots so bad that he hissed again. I swear, it's a good thing that dog doesn't have britches anymore, because he'd definitely be too big for them.

The clump went sailing a good distance, and wouldn't you know, it hit that tree with another *clang*.

Ty puffed his chest up like he was a blowfish. "Did you see that? Just where I said."

"Yeah, but what was that? That wasn't dirt." I started for the tree.

Ty high-fived himself and danced along behind me. I dropped Mr. Boots and let him take the lead on this one. For some reason that clanging dirt was giving me a bad feeling.

Mr. Boots was nosing the big clumps of dirt scattered under the tree when we got there, and one of them in particular seemed to catch his attention. He stopped nosing as we walked up and sat down next to it with a *what the hell* expression on his face. I swear that dog has been watching too much TV. I half-expected him to whip out a notebook and give me his report.

I squatted down next to the clump and poked at it. I was right—there was definitely something non-dirt-like inside the clump. I poked at it again. When it didn't move, explode, or otherwise act dangerous, I figured it was safe, so I swiped at the protective dirt covering enough to figure out what was inside. When I figured it out, I couldn't help but grin. Sometimes I'm way too paranoid.

"Oh Ty, you dork, that wasn't dirt, that was a can."

"What?" Ty wrinkled his forehead and peered at the can. "Okay, fine, but did you see my shot there? That was awesome."

Mr. Boots got a hopeful look in his eyes when he saw it was a can. Tina had recently introduced him to Snausages, and he hasn't been the same since. Kitchen-related items get his salivary glands going.

Never in my life have I been afraid of cans, so I wiped the dirt more vigorously. It looked like it was one of those big metal tea canisters that they sell at the grocery that are supposed to look decorative and nice. Blue and swirly and all. I felt like an archaeologist or something—I mean, who knows what ancient cultures left this can in the lot, right? Okay, since it was a grocery product, it was probably pretty recent, but you never know. It could be valuable.

But as I wiped off the lid, I apparently forgot to use my gentle wiping skills. I knocked off the lid, and the contents of the can came tumbling out onto the grass. I jumped back, almost squashing Mr. Boots in the process. And it's not because I'm afraid of tea, okay? It wasn't tea. It was a skeleton.

CHAPTER 2

OKAY, NOT A BIG ONE OR ANYTHING, BUT A SKELE-
ton just the same. And a bunch of bones are
enough to give anybody the willies. Of course,
Ty didn't have any idea why I suddenly did my
involuntary and highly embarrassing freak-out
dance. Or he didn't until he squatted down and
saw what had fallen out of the canister. Then
he did a pretty embarrassing dance of his own,
I have to say.

"Aw, bones! Eww, Arlie, eww. That's bones!
Those are bones in there!"

Thanks for the news flash, Ty. Like the

hairs on my arms and the back of my neck hadn't already sent me a memo.

The only one who didn't seem freaked out by the whole thing was Mr. Boots. Me and Ty were hovering about five feet away from the can, like we were afraid the bones were going to suddenly reanimate and rush us. But Mr. Boots was taking a pretty healthy interest in the remains. He gave us a disgusted look, muttered something under his breath, and went and stuck his nose into the can. Let me tell you, nothing inspires action like the sight of your dog about to chow down on a mouthful of mystery bones.

"Mr. Boots! No! Drop it!" I lunged for him, managing to grab one hind leg and drag him away from the can. One thing I've got to say, the little guy was a lot more grabbable when he was wearing a confining garment of some sort.

"He's eating it! It's in his mouth!" Ty swayed on his feet and was looking a little woozy. I'd never seen him pass out, but that didn't mean it couldn't happen. I grabbed Mr.

Boots by the face, wrestled his mouth open, and shook him upside down. If there was a tiny skull lurking in there, it was coming out, no two ways about it. I just hoped nothing else belonging to Mr. Boots came out with it.

Mr. Boots held out for a couple of seconds, but then rolled his eyes at me and spit up something white. My stomach rolled over in protest, but I forced myself to look closer. It wasn't a little paw or thigh bone or anything. It was just a piece of paper, like Mr. Boots was some kind of top-secret canine spy destroying evidence. I picked it up and let him go. He immediately stalked off, swearing at me under his breath, and plunked down on the ground to do some serious crotch licking, out of spite I could tell. I ignored him and unfolded the soggy paper. That kind of stuff may work on Mom, but a little crotch licking isn't near enough to get me ruffled.

What I read on the piece of paper was, though.

"Oh no, Ty, we're in trouble here."

Ty wobbled over to me, trying not to look at the bones or Mr. Boots. "What does it say?"

13

"We've been cursed." I held the paper out to him. Written in big block letters across the piece of paper were the words: HERE LIES CUDDLES MCGEE. A CURSE UPON THOSE WHO DISTURB HIS GRAVE. I shuddered involuntarily. One bad decision, one stupid soccer kick, and we were doomed.

Ty looked at the paper for a minute and then handed it back with a shrug. "I don't think we need to worry. It's not like it's real."

I swear, my jaw must've hit the ground. Not a big deal? Sure, maybe I should've just laughed it off. And maybe a year ago I would've. But I've learned to take things like this seriously, and I wasn't about to just shrug it off.

"What? Not real? How can you say that?"

Ty pointed at the bottom of the page. "Because of that."

I looked where Ty was pointing. And, okay, maybe he had a point. Because running along the bottom of the page was curlicue calligraphy saying "From the desk of

Mandy!" with little hearts and butterflies and unicorns prancing next to a ribbon border. Definitely scary, true, and nothing I ever want to see again. But in a gag-me kind of way, not a you're-doomed-for-all-eternity kind of way.

"So you think . . ."

"It's just some kid, Arlie. Someone buried their pet squirrel or rabbit or something."

"Squirrel?"

"You know what I mean. A little pet grave."

A huge raindrop fell onto the note in my hand. The ink of the word "Curse" started to bleed. I shuddered.

"So what do we do with him? With . . ." I looked at the note again. "With Cuddles."

Ty shrugged and squinted up at the sky, catching a huge drop right on the nose. "Well, we either leave the sucker or we get him back in the can and have a funeral tomorrow."

I didn't much like the idea of getting our bony friend back into the can, but I didn't feel right leaving him there, either. He was somebody's pet, somebody's gerbil or kitten or guinea pig or something. Hard to tell, without the skin on.

"Funeral sounds good." Heck, if a funeral is all it takes to avoid a curse, sign me up as the head mourner. "Mr. Boots can be the pall bearer."

Mr. Boots stopped with the crotch licking for a second and gave me a nasty look. I have so had it with that dog's attitude issues.

I used the unicorn-adorned curse to push Cuddles's bones back into the can and we got the lid back on just as the sky opened up.

I snapped on Mr. Boots's Flexi leash, and me and Ty headed for my house at superspeed. Unfortunately, superspeed for us isn't really the dictionary definition of "superspeed," so we were pretty soaked by the time we got there. Add that to the dirt from the construction site and you can pretty much guess how happy my mom was to see us. I'm just glad I'd had the foresight to stash the skeleton can on one of the patio chairs

16

before I headed in. Because if there's one thing that ticks my mom off, it's when I embarrass her in front of company. And when the three of us skittered into the kitchen, we barreled right into Mrs. Knoble from down the street.

"Arlene. And your little black friend. How nice to see you both."

Way to be PC, Mrs. Knoble. I don't know how anyone expects us to do the friendly neighbor routine when she comes out with stuff like that.

Mrs. Knoble did that thing that she does with her mouth sometimes—I think she thinks she's smiling, but it really just looks like she's smelled something disgusting. And usually, that something is me. She doesn't like me on a good day, which makes a lot of my outside time really pleasant, let me tell you. Nothing ruins a good game of live-action lawn Street Fighter like someone watching you from behind the blinds.

Ty has what he calls a Knoble allergy, and he had a pretty immediate reaction. He waved a quick good-bye

17

to everybody, turned, and was halfway down the street before I'd really realized he was leaving.

Apparently, I'd gotten home just in time for Mom and Dad's big departure, because their suitcases were by the door and my sister, Tina, was leaning against the table. I plunked Mr. Boots and the soggy audition announcement down on the kitchen table and tried to clean up a little, but when your hair's plastered to your head, there's only so much you can do.

"Arlie, Mrs. Knoble has agreed to watch you and Tina while we're gone."

Make my day complete, why don't you, Mom? Mrs. Knoble was the last person I wanted watching over me. And I'm serious—I'd rather have Sheriff Shifflett here 24/7 than deal with the Knoblemonster down the street.

"And I've let Sheriff Shifflett know that we're going to be out of town, so he'll be stopping in periodically to make sure everything's okay."

It's like she's some kind of evil mind reader, I'm serious. Mr. Boots is acting out, so she'll punish Arlie for it. It's not my fault their dog's a pervert.

Mr. Boots flopped to his side and reclined against Mom's fruit centerpiece. I could see the place under Mom's eye start to twitch, just like it had when Mrs. Knoble had brought over the *Daily Squealer*'s latest piece on Mr. Boots. He's become the local tabloid paper's favorite topic in the last few months, and their latest pictorial, titled "Boots Gone Wild," was the last straw. She really needed this vacation.

"We're still staying here, though, right?" I have no desire to join the circus, okay? But let it be known— give me a choice between a week at Knoble Central and a lifetime scooping elephant dung and I'm all over that dung. No question.

Lucky for me and the elephants, Mom must've realized that would have been a step too far. "Right. You girls are staying here. But she'll be right down the street if you need anything. This is a total isolation retreat, so that means no phones, no e-mail, no contact at all. Okay, girls? So you need to know you can go to her for anything." Mom nodded at us hopefully. I tried to look agreeable, but I couldn't picture any scenario where I'd willingly go to Mrs. Knoble for help. Tina just shrugged and picked up the flyer from the table.

Mrs. Knoble pursed her lips and did a different thing with her mouth—not quite sure what emotion she was going for there, but it wasn't a good one, I could tell.

"I'll be checking in on you girls at random intervals throughout the day to make sure you're staying out of trouble. So no funny business." Mrs. Knoble squinted at me and Tina like she thought we'd just gotten out of juvie, whipped out her plastic rain bonnet, and headed out without even fastening it under her chin. This week was going to be a joy, I could tell.

Tina had been studying the flyer and suddenly smacked it down on the counter. "I'm doing this."

Mom jumped, that's how on edge she was. "What's that, hon? Doing what?"

"This contest. I'm doing it." She pointed at Mr. Boots. "He's doing it."

Mr. Boots had been lounging against the fruit bowl, sucking on a grape, but even he froze when Tina pointed at him. Sure, he may be nude and lovin' it now, but it wasn't that long ago that Tina was in charge, and the panic in his eyes showed me he hadn't forgotten. I had a feeling his happy life of leisure was over.

Mom went over and took the paper with two fingers. It was still pretty gross looking, I had to admit. "A talent competition? A talent competition for pets?"

Tina rolled her eyes. "No, not a talent competition for pets," she spit, making that sound like the stupidest idea ever to roam the earth. "They're holding auditions to be on *America's Most Talented Pets*. The show? On TV?"

"Oh, on TV." Mom nodded like she knew what Tina was talking about. Mom's not really into TV. I don't think she could've picked that show out if you put it in a lineup with *Friends*, *Jeopardy!*, and the nightly news, but okay, sure.

Tina smirked, like she'd already won a spot. "Mr. Boots is going to totally rock."

Mr. Boots wasn't the only one who was nervous now. As far as I could tell, flaunting your bits doesn't really count as a talent, at least not one I'd ever seen on *America's Most Talented Pets*. And as great as he is, I don't think Mr. Boots has a lot of other skills.

"But . . . uh . . ." Not like I wanted to be the one to break it to her, but it had to be done. "What's he going to do? Does Mr. Boots have a talent?"

Tina glared at me and scooped Mr. Boots off the table. His nostrils were quivering in a way I hadn't seen in months. He knew this was it. Good-bye good times, hello heartache.

"What difference does it make?" Tina said, flinging Mr. Boots up onto her shoulder. "He's awesome, and he's definitely going to win."

A hideous montage flashed through my head: Mr. Boots tap-dancing, Mr. Boots juggling, Mr. Boots jumping through flaming hoops while dressed as the Statue of Liberty. None of them seemed far-fetched. There was no telling what horrors Tina had in mind.

Mom hesitated and opened her mouth to say something, and for a second I thought that Mr. Boots might still have a chance at a normal life. But whatever Mom was going to say, she never got the chance.

Because that's when the patio exploded.

CHAPTER 3

THERE WAS A HUGE FLASH OF LIGHT AND A crackling, crashing noise out back. I swear, if you'd told me our house was being firebombed by crazed Mr. Boots fans desperate to get inside, I would've totally believed you and booked us all a room at the Heather Lodge under a fake name. Maybe under Mr. Marmaduke or Mr. Snoopy or Mr. PleaseGodIDontWantToDie. Whatever. I'm not picky.

Mom screamed, and even Tina looked like she was about to jump out of her skin. Mr. Boots, however, took the opportunity to skedaddle to parts unknown. That dog's no dummy.

"Man, that was close!" Dad came in with another suitcase. If I didn't know better, I'd think they were skipping town for good. "Did you see that lightning? Hooboy!"

"That was lightning?" I'd never seen it hit that close. I have to say, though, I was a little disappointed. Sure, it was scary, but it was just lightning. I thought we were in for major drama here.

"It hit right outside." Mom clutched the table. "Right outside the door." Mom didn't seem to be having any kind of letdown issues—she was still riding the freak-out train.

Dad peered out through the blinds. He frowned. "Man, what did it hit? That just doesn't make sense. The patio furniture's all plastic, so there's no metal to attract— oh my God, the barbecue! Did it get the barbecue?"

Dad jerked the door open and raced out onto the patio. He didn't put on a coat or anything, and it was really coming down out there. He's pretty into his barbecuing. Last year he bought one of those fancy gas models, and he's got a special outfit and everything. (Okay, it's just an apron and a hat. But, still. He's got matching oven mitts.)

"Bill!" Mom screeched, and raced to the door. She stopped in the doorway and bit her lip like Dad had just gone out into the trenches.

Seriously, I don't know what my dad thought he was going to do for the barbecue if it had been hit. It's not like he could nurse it back to health. I don't recall seeing any barbecue repairman certificates in his office. Plus, it was still raining. As far as I know, there's not a one lightning strike per storm rule.

We all huddled around the open door and waited for Dad like we were holding a vigil. All we needed were little candles in paper cups. By the time Dad got back in I was ready to break out in a rendition of "Kumbaya."

Of course, one look at Dad coming inside soaking wet and wielding a pair of barbecue tongs kind of killed that impulse. Dad grinned like a maniac and waved the tongs at us. When I saw what he was holding with the tongs, my stomach fell onto the floor next to my shoes. It was Cuddles's can.

"Barbecue's fine. The lighting was attracted to this."
He held up Cuddles's little metal casket like it was a
trophy and then plunked it down on the granite counter with a flourish. Whatever Cuddles had done in his
life must've been bad, because he was having one lousy
death. We were going to have to throw one heck of a
funeral tomorrow to make up for it. If Cuddles could
make it until tomorrow.

"Now, who wants to tell me what the hell this is?"
Dad poked the can like it was a specimen. It inched a
little closer to the edge of the counter. I had a vision of
the can falling off the counter and little animal bones
scattering all over Mom's formerly clean linoleum. Try
explaining that away.

Time for some fancy footwork. Feet, start moving.
I stepped forward. "Uh, that would be my, uh, project.
For science. You know. A project." I can be a real genius
in the excuse department sometimes. Too bad this wasn't
one of those times.

I reached up, grabbed the tongs away from Dad, and

carefully lifted the can off the counter with them. It was a little blackened on one side, I guess where the lightning had struck it, and seemed to be pretty hot still, but it looked like it was in pretty good shape for all it had been through. Plus that lid seemed nice and secure—I think the lightning may have done a little soldering when it hit. Lightning can be your friend.

"A project?" Dad looked at me, raking his hair back. "For science?" He wrinkled his forehead and stared at me. There was no way I was going to get away with this one. But Dad just sighed and shook his head at me. "Well, Arlie, you're going to have to be a little more careful with your things, okay? That can's all metal, and it was attracting lightning out there. It could've done some serious damage. We're just lucky it didn't hurt that barbecue. Now"—Dad wiped rain off his face—"I'm going to change clothes, and your mother and I are heading out. Put your project away."

"Sure." Didn't have to tell me twice. I raced up the stairs as fast as I could while wielding a pair of barbecue tongs and stashed the can under my bed, well away from my old third-grade composition notebooks. After I determined that the smoking Cuddles can wasn't a fire hazard, I hustled back to the kitchen. Mom and Dad still hadn't made it downstairs, but Tina was just sitting at the table, her chair turned toward the stairs. It was pretty obvious what was going on. She was waiting for me. She knew.

"So. Project, huh?"

I should've known I wouldn't get away with that one. I just nodded.

"So since when are you in summer school?" Tina narrowed her eyes at me suspiciously.

"Since never. So? I don't have to be in school to work on a project." Honestly, I don't even know why I bothered. I was so busted. Tina can sniff out a secret from a mile away.

Tina leaned forward and hissed at me, "You might fool Mom and Dad, but you don't fool me for one second. I don't know what it is you're doing, but as of this

29

minute, you are mine. You hear me? Mine." Did I mention Tina's middle name is "blackmail"?

I figured my options were pretty limited here: cool and casual, which had the chance of throwing her off; or puddle on the floor nervous, which really didn't have any advantages that I could see but was definitely the direction I was leaning. I took a deep breath and tried to go with cool and casual. I flipped my hair and did my best shrug. Of course, my best shrug resembled more of a nervous twitch, but you work with what you have. "It's nothing." Sure, nothing except sucking up to a tiny corpse to escape being doomed for all eternity. No biggie.

Tina pushed back the chair and glared at me, so I'm guessing puddle on the floor would've been a better way to go. She sauntered over to me and got right in my face. I'm serious, I could smell her gum and everything. She's into bubblemint.

"You think I care what your little game is? I don't. But I could still bust you so fast, your head would spin. Just for kicks." Tina paused and smiled at me. Not a friendly *Hey sis, we're buds!* kind of smile, but a *said the spider to the fly* kind of smile.

Tina patted my shoulder. "But I won't. I won't say a word. And in exchange, you do whatever it takes to get Mr. Boots ready for that talent show. Whatever I say, whenever I say."

Forgive me, Mr. Boots. I know not what I do.

"But . . ."

"No buts. You do it. Whatever it takes. That's the deal."

She cracked her gum at me and smirked as Mom and Dad came down the stairs. She threw me a questioning look, raised her eyebrows, and put on her best daughter face. I had approximately three seconds before Tina spilled the beans about my "project," my parents freaked out over my apparent satanic worship of tiny bones, and I was sent to live in Mrs. Knoble's basement for the week as punishment. I had no choice. I was so dead.

"Deal." I was glad Mr. Boots hadn't reappeared since the lightning strike. He'd find out soon enough that I'd sold him out. I didn't need the guilt trip right now.

Mom and Dad said their good-byes and gave us instructions and gushed and hugged and everything, but I didn't hear a thing they said—all I could think about was the millions of ways that Tina was going to make my life miserable while they were gone. Add that to how ticked Mr. Boots was going to be and Mrs. Knoble creeping around spying on me, and let me tell you, the inside of Cuddles's can was starting to look pretty appealing. Maybe the little guy had a spare room.

Tina apparently decided to torture me with waiting instead of doing anything right away—after our parents left, she just headed upstairs, went into her room, and slammed the door. I'm no masochist, I wasn't going to hang around just waiting for the abuse to start, so I headed up to my room and went to bed. There was always the chance Tina would forget about her plans overnight, right?

I changed into my pajamas and checked to make sure the can was still there. It hadn't moved, but it did look like it had cooled off a little, so I tried to open it up to peek inside. You know, make sure Cuddles was tucked in tight. But it wouldn't budge—that lightning had welded the lid on, and since I didn't have a blowtorch handy, I wasn't going to be getting inside. Which was just fine by me. I'd seen enough of those bones for one lifetime. I stashed the can back under the bed, crawled under the covers, and went to sleep.

Or that was the plan, at least. Trust me to fail miserably at even that. I couldn't drop off, and when I did, I would suddenly jerk awake—it was really creepy. The first time, I felt like somebody was watching me, but when I turned on the light and checked, there wasn't anyone else there. I did find Mr. Boots in a shoebox in the back of my closet, but his eyes were shut tight, so I don't think he was sneaking peeks at me.

The next time I woke up, I couldn't breathe. It felt like there was something heavy sitting on my chest. I bolted out of bed and snapped on the light, but again, nothing. (Mr. Boots had emerged from the shoebox but was now firmly ensconced in a furry slipper I got in sixth grade.) After I convinced myself I was just imagining things, I fell back asleep, but then I woke up with the sheets feeling all clammy and weird. It was always something.

The last time was the last straw, though. I don't know if you've ever woken up with a Chihuahua's foot in your nose, but if you haven't, let me just assure you, it's not pleasant. I don't know what was up with Mr. Boots. It was like he'd tried to crawl inside my nostril during the night, gotten ankle deep, realized he wouldn't fit, and thought, *Well, what the heck, good enough*. That was it for me. I had to get some sleep.

I did a quick assessment of the room and, with infallible half-asleep logic, I decided Cuddles's can was to blame. It was the only thing that was new, and it had to go. Sure, it didn't make any sense, and yeah, I pretty much knew that, but when you're half asleep, you do all kinds of crazy things. I stomped downstairs with the can and stashed it behind the kitchen trash bin. It would be safe enough there until we held the funeral tomorrow. And it's not like there was any chance Tina would take out the trash in the meantime.

I stomped back upstairs and found Mr. Boots buried under the pillow. The only reason I even knew he was there was that I could see his nostrils quivering under the ruffle at the edge. I dragged the little guy out by a leg and crawled back into bed. I was asleep before Mr. Boots even stopped cussing me out.

Moving the can seemed to do the trick, because the sun was up when I woke up again. Mr. Boots was sprawled at the foot of my bed, waving his feet in his sleep. Now that I was using awake-person logic, I felt a little bad about kicking Cuddles out of my room. It's not like it was his fault I couldn't sleep. Plus, I couldn't stop the nagging fear that Tina would find that can and Cuddles would end up a little bony hostage. Not that I could figure out what she would do to him now that Mom and Dad were gone, but I didn't want to take the chance. Tina is nothing if not creative.

I padded downstairs to get the can, partially motivated by thoughts of Tina, but also thinking that an early morning Twinkie might be in order. Retrieve the can, get a Twinkie, maybe a Snausage for Mr. Boots, head back up to bed. It was good to have a plan.

That was before I went into the kitchen.

Now, I've seen pictures on TV of places that have been hit by tornadoes. And pictures of towns that have had a hurricane go through. So I know what an official disaster area is supposed to look like. Believe me, if I could've gotten a government inspector to come to our kitchen, it would've qualified. The place was trashed, and I'm not exaggerating.

Every single cabinet had been opened, and it looked like every box in there had been thrown into the middle of the floor and shredded. Forget Twinkies, Snausages—they were history, along with the crackers, boxes of cereal, potato chips, everything. I'd never seen anything like it. The curtains were hanging by the rods in shreds, like someone had tried to make a paper snowflake or paper doll, messed up, and taken out their rage on the rest of the fabric.

Mr. Boots had come down the stairs behind me and he waded out into the middle of the room with a horrified expression on his face, like he'd just missed the party of the year. I waded out after him, trying to take in the carnage. It was then that I noticed the door. It looked like the bottom corner had been torn off piece by piece, and big, jagged chunks were lying scattered around the trash can. That's when I remembered Cuddles. I raced over and looked behind the trash can. Cuddles's can was still there, but it was lying on its side and the lid was lying next to it. The lid that had been firmly welded on the night before.

I grabbed the can and looked inside. I felt like I was going to be sick. It was empty.

CHAPTER 4

I TRIED TO MAKE SENSE OF EVERYTHING. THAT lid had been soldered on by the lightning—I'd tested it myself. I didn't know what had come through our house, ruined Cuddles's can, and destroyed our kitchen, and I wasn't sure I wanted to know. I was still staring at the can in my hand when Tina showed up in the doorway.

"What the—"

It was almost worth it, just to see Tina's jaw hit the floor like that. She's gotten pretty good at maintaining a calm and collected façade (read: bored and above it all), and on occasion

I've tried to figure out scenarios that would make her totally lose it. You know, like when I'm waiting in the lunch line, or having my teeth cleaned, or whenever. But I never figured that bringing a can of moldy old bones into the house would do the trick. Heck, if I had, I might've tried it years ago. Okay, not really. But it was still pretty awesome.

"Mr. Boots? Oh, Mr. Boots!" Tina slammed her hands onto her hips so hard, I was afraid she was going to dislocate something. "Bad Mr. Boots! Bad dog!" Tina pointed at Mr. Boots like she was a witness in a courtroom TV show, quivering finger and everything. Mr. Boots, who had been happily snuffling through the pile of shredded paper, froze and stared at me with a horrified expression.

Tina was shaking her head so hard, I thought she'd give herself whiplash. "No, Mr. Boots, no! Arlie, how could you let him do that?"

Me and Mr. Boots, all we could do was stare at each other. I don't think either one of us expected him to get the blame for this one. Because where blame is concerned, this was huge. He's a Chihuahua, for goodness' sakes. He has a bite the size of a Wheat Thin. He didn't even look the part. The poor guy had a piece of napkin stuck to his lip.

I shrugged and tried to laugh it off. Like the total destruction of the kitchen was some tiny thing, no big deal. "Mr. Boots? Come on, Tina, it wasn't him." I shrugged again and tried to think of some non-Boots-related reason for the carnage. I was a pretty lousy alibi witness, it's true. But it didn't matter. Tina had obviously made up her mind.

"I cannot BELIEVE you let him do this, Arlie. Mom and Dad are going to freak when they hear about it. And I don't even want to think about what this is going to do to his chances in the talent competition. Nobody wants a vandal for a winner, Arlie. I watch TV, okay, and delinquents get disqualified. This canNOT get out. Oh, my God, he did that to the door?"

The piece of napkin fluttered to the floor as Mr.

Boots whipped around to look at the door. The hole was three times bigger than he was. It would've taken him three years and some extra sets of teeth to manage that kind of destruction. He looked too shocked to even bolt. It was a lot to take in.

"Yeah well, it's not as bad as it looks. I'll fix it. A little Spackle and nobody'll ever know," I stammered, moving to block the gaping hole from Tina's laservision. Spackle, right. Spackle can work wonders, sure, but it has to have something to stick to. You can't spackle air.

"Well, you better." She gave me a glare that would've disintegrated the rest of the door if she hadn't been carefully aiming it at me. "And he," she said, scooping Mr. Boots up with one hand, "is coming with me. Somebody obviously has too much energy. Somebody needs to channel it into developing his talent." She swung him over her shoulder and marched upstairs. Mr. Boots worked his mouth as he disappeared up the stairs, but he couldn't even manage a squeak of protest. I didn't blame him—it had all happened too fast. I'd been awake, what, five minutes? I hadn't even gotten my eyelashes unstuck yet.

I grabbed the broom and dustpan while I dialed the phone. Ty had some serious explaining to do. If this wasn't a curse, I didn't know what it was. It took a couple of tries, but eventually I woke him up, and once he'd heard about the unexpected renovation of our kitchen, he was out the door like a shot. I'd still managed to fill three trash bags with the remains of our kitchen before he got there, though.

"Whoa," Ty said, tramping through my neatly arranged piles of shredded paper. "This is seriously messed up."

"No kidding." I tried to sweep the paper bits back into a pile, but it wasn't working. I was doing more angry whacking than gentle sweeping, and that's just not very effective.

"Man, we shouldn't have laughed. That Mandy sure knows her stuff. Remind me not to get on her bad side," Ty snorted, picking up the remains of a Twinkie box.

I looked at it sadly. "I think we already did. So, who do you think did this?"

Ty looked at me like I'd grown an extra head. An extra stupid head. "What do you mean? We know who did this."

"Huh?" Maybe the one head I had was stupid enough. I just wasn't getting it. And seriously, if I had to hear one more person blame Mr. Boots, I was going to lose it.

"Cuddles, Arlie. Remember him? Cuddles is obviously one ticked-off bony thing. I'm thinking a rat. Like one of those superrats? The kind that can eat through concrete? They have tempers, from what I hear. And man, that's one ticked-off dead rat."

Apparently I'd have to get in the losing-it line, because Ty had just cut to the front. I sighed and tried to use my calming voice. You know, the one for little kids and crazy people. "Ty, Cuddles is a skeleton. Cuddles is a pile of little bones. And he's not even here! His can is empty!"

Ty gave me a sassy nod. I hate it when he does that.

He thinks he's so cool. I'm surprised he didn't snap. "Exactly, Arlie. Cuddles is not here. Cuddles has fled the scene." Ty was using his calming voice too. My broom hand was starting to itch. I controlled it.

"Ty, bones aren't mobile. Cuddles can't go anywhere on his own. He was kidnapped. Something busted in here, grabbed him, and took off." As the words came out, though, I was already having doubts. Who breaks in and trashes a place to steal a skeleton? How much sense does that make? And besides me and Ty, who even knew Cuddles was here? "Besides, I don't think Mandy's the rat type."

At least I didn't have doubts about that. I'm sorry, but unicorns and little hearts don't say "rat" to me. I was thinking fuzzy bunny. Cuddles the bunny—that had a nice ring to it. I could totally buy that. And, yeah, I know there are ear issues, since I didn't recall seeing any long, bunny-ear-shaped bones, but maybe the ears don't have bones? I've never done a comparative study of animal skeletons, so sue me.

44

Ty frowned and hauled himself up onto the kitchen island, his feet dangling. Normally, I would've said something about that because Ty's butt on the food preparation area is something that would cause a major Mom freak out. But since the island had gnaw marks all up and down the sides, I figured Ty's butt was the least of my problems. I held my tongue.

Ty was starting to look uneasy, anyway. "Huh. You're right. Rats aren't cute, are they? And Mandy seems like a cute type. Maybe Cuddles was a white rat? Those are cute, right? Well, cute-ish. A little. Except for those red eyes . . ."

"It wasn't Cuddles, okay?" I threw the broom down. I wasn't going to be Nancy McNeaterson while everyone else was off dangling their feet and learning dog tricks and whatnot. "It couldn't be. Right?"

Ty shrugged. "Well, it doesn't matter. The good news is, if it *was* him, he's gone now. And if it wasn't him, whatever did it is gone now too." Ty pointed at the missing chunk of door, explaining like I was in preschool. "Cuddles trashed the place and took off, or the Cuddles liberator took off, whatever. Either way, you're good. We'll just do a little bit of tidying and no one will ever know he was here. Problem solved."

I had a feeling it wasn't going to be that easy, but who knows, right? Not everything has to turn into an issue. I have to admit, it did make me feel better to have those bones out of the house. And as a bonus, it was what Dad would call "a good learning experience." Thanks to Cuddles, I can now cross "mortician" off of my list of future career possibilities. Thanks, Cuddles.

I had gotten most of the trash back into what I like to call piles when Tina came stomping through the kitchen, Mr. Boots jostling up and down on her shoulder like he was on some kind of human pogo stick. It didn't look healthy—his eyes were even starting to roll back in his head. I think he was trying to make himself pass out. I couldn't really blame him, though. I often have the same reaction to Tina.

Tina chucked Mr. Boots onto the floor, where he promptly crawled into a half-chewed saltines box and scooted it into a corner. Tina thrust a piece of paper at me. It was a list. A long one.

"What's this? It's not your birthday, Tina."

Tina rolled her eyes. "Supplies, Arlie. Mr. Boots isn't going to win this contest on his looks alone. He needs props. You're going to get them."

I scanned the list doubtfully. I wasn't sure where I was going to be able to find a pair of dog-size pom-poms. "I don't know, Tina. . . ."

Tina sighed like I was the biggest doofus she'd ever seen and handed me a wad of money. "The Pet Emporium, Arlie? That's where you get dog supplies. Now get going—every second Mr. Boots isn't rehearsing is a second wasted."

Ty peered at the list over my shoulder. "Do they carry fire batons at the Pet Emporium?"

Tina acted like Ty hadn't even said a word. "If he loses, it's on your head, Arlie. I know what I'm doing.

47

Now, GO!" Tina put one hand on my shoulder and one hand on Ty's and physically shoved us out the door. "Don't make me say it again."

She didn't have to tell me twice. I'm no dummy—every minute spent at the Pet Emporium was a minute not spent cleaning that kitchen. And besides, I heard her throw the deadbolt in the door behind us, so it's not like I had much choice. Sure, I wished I'd brushed my teeth and wasn't still wearing my pajama top, but sometimes you have to make sacrifices. And if I was lucky, maybe by the time we got back, Tina would have forgotten that she'd put "Chihuahua tap shoes" on the list. I don't care what she said, I had a hard time believing they carried them downtown.

I tried the door to verify—yup, locked—grinned sheepishly at Ty, and raked my fingers through my hair to do a little impromptu detangling. Mom's gone, what, eight hours? And already my grooming practices are shot. But it's not like I'd be seeing anybody, right?

Or at least that's what I thought until I heard the

heels tapping on our driveway. These days, there's only one person in our neighborhood who wears high heels day and night. And that person was already out for my blood. And, thanks to Mom, I was powerless to resist.

I tossed my head, hoping I just had the nicely tousled look and not the rat's-nest-does-this-girl-ever-bathe? look, and smiled up at Mrs. Knoble.

I don't know why I even bothered. She twisted her mouth around like she'd accidentally gotten a chunk of lemon in her fruit salad and clutched her purse a little tighter. "Arlene. And Tyrone. How nice."

Ty shifted uncomfortably and gave a half wave. "Hey, Mrs. Knoble. I . . . er . . . hey."

Boy, did I wish I wasn't wearing that pajama top. I felt like it had BEDCLOTHES written on it in huge letters on the front and ARLENE JACOBS ISN'T EVEN CAPABLE OF DRESSING HERSELF on the back. But heck, who needs words, right? If there's a universal symbol that screams "pajamas," I'm pretty sure it's the smiling duck wearing fuzzy pink slippers and a bathrobe that I had emblazoned on my front. I folded my arms and tried to pretend like slipper ducks were the height of teen fashion.

"I'm glad you're up and about, Arlene. I came by to discuss some basic ground rules with you and your sister."

"Ground rules?" I don't know why I asked—I so didn't want to know.

"Curfews, appropriate activities—that sort of thing. Just because your parents are away, don't think I'm going to let you girls run wild. Now, if you'll excuse us, Tyrone? I don't know that Arlene should be having male visitors."

Mrs. Knoble pursed her lips at him and grabbed hold of my upper arm to lead me inside in a friendly way that I was sure was going to leave a mark.

I glanced at the door and suddenly had an image of Mrs. Knoble standing in our chewed-up, totally destroyed kitchen. It wasn't a pretty image. It involved a lot of screaming, some carnage, and Tina and me locked up in juvie for the next week. This called for some fancy thinking.

"I would love to, Mrs. Knoble, but I've got to get downtown." I held up Tina's list and then folded it up and stashed it in my pocket. All it would take to spoil my plan was for Mrs. Knoble to accidentally see the words "sequined top hat." "I've got to get to the pharmacy. It's Tina, she's not feeling so good."

Mrs. Knoble hesitated, and I could actually see little flashes of thoughts running across her face. It was either that or some kind of nervous twitch. I like to give her the benefit of the doubt.

Mrs. Knoble seemed to settle on a thought. Unfortunately for me, it was the wrong one. She put on a sympathetic face, kind of like the ones in those sad-clown paintings. "Oh, the poor dear. Let me go to her. She'll need an adult to take care of her."

This was not going the way I had hoped. Thankfully, Ty was working backup.

"You don't want to do that, ma'am," Ty said. "Arlie means real sick. Like stomach sick. Intestinal problems sick. Sick sick."

"It's pretty messy in there," I said truthfully.

More flashes across the face. "Oh. I see. Not a fever?"

Ty shook his head gravely. I held my breath.

Mrs. Knoble hesitated. It was a tough decision, I could tell. She'd get bonus points for being the responsible, caring adult, but gross bodily functions were pretty much a dealbreaker. In the end, the ick factor won out.

"Well, if you're sure she'll be okay? I would go in, but I don't want to embarrass the poor girl."

"She'll be fine. I just need to get her the medicine. That's all. No big deal." I leaned in conspiratorially. "This happens to Tina all the time. She's got the weakest stomach I've ever seen. She's notorious in school. Can hardly get through the day without yuking all over something. I'm surprised you've never noticed it."

"They're doing a study for some medical journal. It's a pretty rare condition. She might be on *Oprah*," Ty added. A little unnecessarily, I thought. I didn't want to overplay this.

"Oprah?" Mrs. Knoble's eyes lit up like a beacon. Thanks a lot, Ty.

"Not Oprah. That's not happening. Oprah passed. Didn't want to mess up the studio, you know." I shot Ty a dirty look.

"Yes, of course." Mrs. Knoble pinched her face up in some way that I'd never seen before. It was like she was working muscles in her face that didn't usually see any action. I wonder if she practices in a mirror. Finally she came to a decision. "Well, you tell her to call me if she needs anything at all. I'll be right down the street and I'm happy to come over. We can lay down the ground rules when everyone's feeling up to it."

I nodded and tried not to smirk as Mrs. Knoble gave me and Ty one last once-over and scuttled away across the street.

I couldn't believe we'd gotten away with it. As soon as I knew she wasn't coming back, I pointed to my lame pajama top. "Seriously, it looks like a T-shirt?" I cringed at the sound of my voice—I totally sounded like I was begging.

Ty gave me a weak smile. "Yeah. Totally. You look great."

It was so obvious that he was lying, but I was willing to take it. I know—pathetic, right?

I grabbed Ty and booked it toward town. Because I knew one thing for sure—Mrs. Knoble might be gone, but she wasn't going to be gone for long.

CHAPTER 5

MY HEART DIDN'T STOP RACING UNTIL WE'D made it to the pet store. Oh wait, excuse me, Knoble's Pet Emporium. The Knobles get really ticked off when you don't call their stores by their proper names.

They moved into town a couple of years ago and right away they started buying up everything that didn't move and plastering their name all over it. Now it's Knoble's Pet Emporium, Knoble's Happy Mart, and the grocery is the Knoblemart. Apparently they're loaded.

Mom says it's some kind of not-having-kids

issue, but I think the Knobles are just jerks. I can say that as their neighbor, right? Because I should get some perks for having to live down the street from them. What I can't figure out, though, is why are they living in my neighborhood? It's okay, don't get me wrong, but it's not fancy or anything. Personally, I think they're trying to drive everyone on our street crazy so that they can buy up all the houses for cheap and build themselves some kind of Knobles-only retreat. Mom says I'm being silly, but come on, why else would they put up with Mr. Boots lounging on their front porch every morning showing off his bits? (Because that's kind of become a routine with him. Not that I officially know about it, because if Mom finds out, I am so dead.)

And seriously, that's kind of what happened with Ace, down at the pet store. (Not the bits part, although I'm sure he's seen his share.) Word on the street is that Mr. Knoble went to the store every single day to convince Ace to sell, and finally Ace just caved. I'm surprised he lasted as long as he did. I don't think I'd last one week with Mr. Knoble constantly in my face. Ty thinks that Mr. Knoble must've had something on Ace for him to give in so easily. But then Ty is convinced that the guy down at Knoble's Olde-Tyme Ice Cream Shoppe is a secret agent because of his shifty eyes and penetrating stare, so take that for what it's worth.

I have to admit, though, the Knobles did more than just change the name. Ace's pet store always felt really dark and crowded and a little bit sketchy, like the fish in back were up to no good. And when you went inside, hooboy, did you know you were in a pet store. The Emporium is a lot brighter, and it has more of a hospital smell, which I guess is an improvement. The fish seem to have cleaned up their act too, and now they just swim around minding their own business.

One thing I really can't stand about the new place, though—they added a bell. And not just a regular "tinkle tinkle" bell either.

I took a deep breath to prepare myself and opened the door. Immediately there was a huge blare of parade music from above the door, followed immediately by Mr. Knoble's whiny nasal voice. "WELCOME TO KNOBLE'S PET EMPORIUM, WHERE PETS COME TO PARTY." Yeah, it makes no sense. No matter how hard Mr. Knoble tries, he's just not going to be cool. Sad, if you ask me.

Ricky Burgess was working at the counter, and he flinched noticeably as we walked in. I don't blame him. If I had to hear Mr. Knoble's party welcome every ten minutes, I think I'd lose it and start juggling gerbils or something.

Ricky recovered quickly and gave us a quick wave. Everybody in town knows Ricky, mostly because most people went to school with him at one point or another. He's failed tenth grade about a million times. He was a couple of years ahead of Tina when we first met him, then he was in Tina's class, but I think he finally dropped out to go full time at the Emporium when he saw my class in his future. He never let it get him down, though, so it didn't seem like the huge bummer that it probably was. And heck, days at the Emporium are probably less stressful than facing another sophomore year of high school.

I tore Tina's list in half and gave part of it to Ty. This was going to be interesting.

Ty looked at his half of the list and shot me a dirty look. "Oh, thanks, Arlie. Give me the half with the hard stuff on it. 'Flaming batons?' Sure, no problem."

I rolled my eyes at him. "Yeah, sorry, Ty. I should've given you my easy list instead. Now, if you'll excuse me, I have to get the flaming hoops for Mr. Boots to jump through."

Ty shook his head. "That dog is in for a serious heinie burn."

"Tell me about it." I had a bad feeling that Ty was right. Mr. Boots was not exactly model-quality right now, if you catch my drift. Add a couple of disfiguring burns and he could audition for the part of Frankenstein's dog in the school play. (Except I think the fall play is supposed to be some musical, *The Sound of Music*, maybe. Even so, it would be pretty awesome if Frankenstein's dog made a surprise appearance and kicked some Nazi butt.)

I gathered as many of the things on my list as I could, but no surprise, there were some things that they didn't seem to carry. I managed to find little barrels to balance on, I got the tiny wire for the high-wire act, and I settled on some parakeet swings to use as flaming hoops. I figured all it would take is a little lighter fluid and those suckers would light right up. But I think it was pretty unrealistic of Tina to think I would find the tap shoes and starter pistol.

Ty still seemed to be looking for things, so I headed over to the pet section to do a little investigative work. Since I'd seen Cuddles without his skin, it wouldn't be that hard to imagine what he'd look like with it on, right? It'd be like imagining someone in a new outfit.

I ruled out the mice right away—way too small, and isn't there a bone in that tail? I didn't remember Cuddles having a tail. That seemed to be key, because it ruled out the ferrets, kittens, and gerbils.

The hamsters fit the no-tail criteria, but they looked pretty puny, so I figured I'd been right all along. Cuddles had to be a bunny. I was peering into the rabbit cage, trying to answer the eternal ear/bone question, when Ty showed up.

"Man, Arlie, Tina's going to kill you. I couldn't find flaming batons anywhere. Think she'll be satisfied with the juggle balls and hurtles?"

"Doubt it." I sighed. Ty peered into the rabbit cage too, and then shook his head. "No way. That rabbit's not right—the feet are all wrong. I don't think Cuddles was a rabbit."

Talk about spending too much time with a person. It was creepy how Ty knew just what I was thinking. Besides, what did it matter what Cuddles was, anyway? Ty was right, he was long gone.

"Forget it, let's just get this stuff to Tina."

We piled our loot in front of Ricky and he nodded knowingly as he scanned them. *"America's Most Talented Pets,* huh? I can see the signs. So who's the lucky pet?"

"Mr. Boots," I said, handing him the top hat I'd found. "I'm not sure what his talent is yet, though."

"Mr. Boots?" Ricky's smile faded a little. "Your Chihuahua? That dog in the paper?"

"Yeah." I hoped he wasn't about to bust on our dog. Sure, he wasn't that coordinated, but he was still an okay dog. And a town celebrity, if you believed the *Daily Squealer.* "He'll be great."

"I'll bet." Ricky nodded, and smiled back again. "If Tina's coaching him, he'll have to do well, right?

"Right." Like I said, Ricky's been around awhile; he knows how things are.

"So, Ricky." Ty cleared his throat. "Hypothetical question here, okay? Say your pet makes a huge mess. Torn up paper, things chewed up, that kind of thing. What kind of pet would you say that was?"

Ricky stopped scanning and chewed on his lip while he thought. "Well, could be lots of things. Chewing and tearing, dogs do that. Cats do more scratching, so probably not a cat. Rodents, they're constantly chewing—

they have to, to keep their teeth worn down. So it could be a rodent. Probably not a fish." Ricky grinned at me and started scanning the juggling balls.

"Thanks for narrowing that down," Ty grumbled. "So Arlie, that settles that, Cuddles is definitely a dog or a rodent."

"Cuddles?"

Ricky went pale and dropped one of the balls. It bounced off the counter and rolled over by the pig-ear bin, but he didn't even seem to notice.

"Cuddles McGee?"

Ty and I glanced at each other nervously. I'd never seen anybody so pale. Ricky was practically transparent. I swear, I could see his veins and everything.

"Maybe. You know Cuddles McGee?" I was seriously hoping there were two Cuddles McGees running around out there.

"I thought he was dead." Ricky swayed a little.

"Well, that checks out. This Cuddles is dead. The one we're thinking of."

I'm serious, when I said that, you could actually see Ricky relax. The color just went gushing back into his face, turning him a healthy pink. Actually, maybe a little pinker than usual, because I think he was embarrassed.

"Oh, well, of course. Cuddles McGee. He's no big deal, just this hamster we had in here once, when I was just part time. We boarded him."

Hamster? Yeah, right. Thanks to my handy investigative work, I knew he had the wrong Cuddles.

"Oh, well, this couldn't be the same Cuddles. The Cuddles we're talking about is a LOT bigger than a hamster. He's huge." I gave a relieved smile. Bones don't lie, right?

Ricky frowned at me and shook his head. "I don't know. Cuddles McGee was the biggest hamster I've ever seen. Gigantic. Like he ate other hamsters for breakfast big. When Mandy brought him in here to board, I told her—"

"Mandy?" My heart stopped for a minute. Cuddles was really a hamster?

"Mandy McGee. When she brought him in to board, I told her she was feeding him wrong. Normal hamsters don't eat meat, but you should've seen Cuddles attack a plate of bacon. That might be what made him so huge. And mean! I tried to change his water and he practically took my finger off. One time when Ace took the lid off the cage, Cuddles jumped him and went for the jugular. I just threw his seeds in the cage and slammed the lid down after that. Mandy asked Ace to clean the cage, but when she got back he told her, sorry, not without a tranquilizer gun. We had to ask her not to bring him back. It upset the other animals too much."

This, naturally, was exactly what I wanted to hear. Nothing like hearing that the cursed bones you've disturbed belong to a gigantic mutant killer hamster.

Ricky just stared down at the scanner in his hand like he was having some kind of traumatic flashback.

"Yeah, well, good thing he's dead, huh," Ty said after a minute. Ricky nodded and stuck the last of Tina's implements of torture into the bag. He was looking a little white around the mouth again.

"Yeah good thing." He handed me the bag. "Well, good luck. I hope Mr. Boots gets on TV."

"Thanks." I took the bag and started toward the door.

I know Cuddles was gone and not my problem anymore, but I have to admit that I was just a wee bit freaked out, you know? There was that gaping hole in our kitchen door. Anything could get in.

I turned back to Ricky. "Mandy McGee. Do you know where she lives? If I wanted to talk to her?"

Ricky nodded. "She's up on Old Orange Road, out by the school. I think her mom remarried—it's Mandy Burke now."

I nodded and hustled out as parade music blared from over the door. Ty grabbed my arm as soon as we hit the pavement.

"What, you think Mandy knows something? 'Cause I don't think we need to talk to her. I think we're okay with the curse. It's over."

I was getting sick of people grabbing my arm. "I just wanted to know. In case, all right?"

Ty shook his head. "Man, I am sick of evil hamsters and ticked-off sisters. What I need is to go to the Happy Mart for a Happy Dog. Sound good? 'Cause after that, I'm heading home."

Coward. I wasn't particularly looking forward to telling Tina we hadn't been able to find most of the stuff on the list either, but it's not like I could avoid it. Thanks for skipping out on me, buddy. But I couldn't really blame him. "Sure. A Happy Dog would be great."

We headed over to Knoble's Happy Mart and went inside. But I regretted it the second we set foot in the building. Because standing at the counter was none other than my biggest fan, Sheriff Shifflett.

He's had it out for me ever since our little run-in last spring, and I think he blames me for his bad poll numbers. He's supposedly running for re-election, but his numbers dropped hugely after the prom, and he doesn't even seem to be campaigning anymore. It's like he's given up completely.

Luck seemed to be with me, though, because Sheriff Shifflett didn't even notice we'd come in. He was fixated instead on the clerk behind the counter. And from the way steam seemed to be coming out of his ears, we hadn't caught him wearing his happy face.

"This is a Happy Mart, isn't it?" Sheriff Shifflett was stabbing his fleshy finger into the chest of the Happy Mart checkout guy. Hard. "And Happy Mart serves Happy Dogs, doesn't it?" The guy stared in google eyed terror at Sheriff Shifflett's finger. It was like he'd never seen a finger before and didn't know why it was attacking him.

"Yes, sir." The clerk swallowed hard. I wasn't sure what to do. It was kind of like watching a stickup. I didn't know whether to try to help or run like hell. I was leaning toward run like hell.

Shifflett wasn't even close to finished, though. "Then maybe you can explain to me why in the hell this HAPPY MART doesn't seem to have any HAPPY DOGS. Does this make sense to you, son?"

Aha. I noticed the Happy Dog heater on the end of the counter, looking lonely and sad without any Happy Dogs inside. The clerk looked like he was going to throw up on Sheriff Shifflett's finger. "We ran out," he squeaked.

"Ran out? How the hell does a Happy Mart run out of Happy Dogs?"

Well, that did it for me. Decision made. No Happy Dogs equals no reason for me to be there. Verdict: Run like hell.

Of course that was the exact moment that Ty chose to clear his throat.

Sheriff Shifflett's head whipped around so fast, I thought it would fly off and bounce off the door behind me.

"Oh, hey, Sheriff," I said weakly.

His eyes narrowed as he glared at me and Ty. He stopped poking the clerk and sauntered over. The clerk visibly wilted, slumping against the counter like that podgy finger had been the only thing holding him up.

"Well, if it isn't one of the Jacobs girls." Sheriff Shifflett had never been great at remembering my name. Not that I minded, though. "Your mother tells me I need to keep an eye on you for a while."

"That's right."

"You staying out of trouble? Or are you up to your old tricks again?"

Well, that didn't seem quite fair to me, especially since I was the one who had basically saved the town a couple of months ago, but I kept my mouth shut. No point in antagonizing him—especially when he was already in a mood—that's what I was thinking.

I held up the Pet Emporium bag. "We just went down to the Pet Emporium for some stuff for our dog," I said in what I hoped was my most innocent voice.

Sheriff Shifflett just stared at me. I did a mental rewind and went back over what I'd said, just to make sure I hadn't accidentally admitted to robbing the place or something. Because it totally felt like Shifflett was trying to decide whether to arrest me now or after he got his Happy Dog. Thankfully, Ty's a master at working situations like this.

"Yeah, got some dog supplies," he said. "And then, we thought, man, wouldn't a Happy Dog really hit the spot right now? So we came over, but I guess we're out of luck. I can't believe they're out of Happy Dogs. How does something like that even happen?"

The clerk shot Ty the nastiest look I've ever seen, even from Tina, and that's really saying something. But it was too late. The damage was done.

"That is exactly what I was trying to determine," Sheriff Shifflett boomed, turning back to the clerk. He had bigger fish to fry than Arlie Jacobs. "No Happy Dogs. And at a Happy Mart! Never heard of such a thing. And you know what? I think that sounds criminal, that's what I think. False advertising. Deceiving the public. Sounds to me like a criminal offense."

Ty nodded and jerked the door open. "Definitely. It's

insane. Good thing you're here, Sheriff. 'Bye!"

Ty pushed me out onto the sidewalk as he slammed the door shut behind me. I went skittering across the pavement and almost barreled right into the Happy Hog statue out front. And trust me, a giant seven-foot plastic statue of a pig wearing a vest and chef's hat is not something you want to accidentally slam into. I don't care how spiffy he looks.

"Man, that was mean," I said, shooting Ty a disapproving look.

"Sometimes you have to save yourself." Ty grinned at me. "Remember that when you see Tina. My advice— do like Ricky did with Cuddles. Throw the bag and run like hell."

He gave me a lazy high five and headed off down the street toward his house.

I reminded myself again that I didn't mind Ty ditching me and headed home. (Because let's face it, Ty's a ditcher. That's the way of the world. If I let it get to me, we would've stopped being friends years ago, probably around second grade, when we decided to play piñata party with the cool dangly thing in the tree. Ty was heading for the hills before the bees had even decided the girl with the stick was enemy number one. To be fair, he did come back with my dad and calamine lotion.)

I was prepared for fireworks when I walked into the house, but not the kind I got.

Mr. Boots was standing in the middle of the kitchen table on a piece of paper, with his feet covered in paint. The front feet were red and green, and the back feet were blue and yellow. He'd hunched up his back like he was trying to get as far away from those feet as possible, and he gave me a desperate pleading look.

"So, what's all this?" I said, holding the bag out to Tina.

She snatched it away from me. "Oh Arlie, thank GOD. I don't know what I'm going to do with him! I thought Mr. Boots could do some painting as a talent, but just look at him!"

I did. Mr. Boots stretched a little taller. It didn't work, though—he was still firmly attached to his feet.

"His paintings aren't good?" I wasn't seeing the problem here. Animal paintings are never good, are they?

"They aren't even paintings!" Tina spat, holding up paper after paper. Each one was blank except for four tiny footprints. "He won't even move! I keep trying to get him to shuffle around or walk or ANYTHING, but no, he just stands there like a freak!"

Mr. Boots did look a little like a freak, I have to admit. But I think it was more the look of anguish on his face and the colorful feet, and those were definitely Tina's fault. "Well, those are kind of nice."

Tina crumpled the papers in fury and threw them into the corner at the trash can. It looked like Tina had bagged up most of the destroyed kitchen piles and dumped them on the trash can, so now the destruction was contained in one area. Mr. Boots's bad art bounced off one of the bags and landed near the door.

"Nice?" Tina growled. "Standing on a piece of paper

is not a talent, Arlie. He's not going to win with pictures of his damn footprints."

She definitely had a point there.

"Never mind." She grabbed Mr. Boots with one hand and the bag with the other and stomped upstairs. She was getting paint all over her shirt, but I didn't think this was the time to mention it. "We'll be in my room. Don't bother us. We're not coming out until Mr. Boots shows some actual talent." She never even looked in the bag.

I waited until she was gone and then made myself a sandwich. I hung around the kitchen for a little while, waiting for Tina to show up and ream me out for forgetting some of the supplies, but she didn't show. All I heard were periodic bouts of cursing coming from her room.

I used the powerstapler to staple a big piece of cardboard in front of the hole in the door as a temporary fix and then headed up to my room. If Tina wanted to yell at me, she'd have to wait.

There were a couple of Twinkies lying on my pillow,

which I guess Tina must have salvaged when she bagged the trash earlier. It was pretty nice of her to give them to me—she totally could've kept them for herself, because I hadn't even realized any had survived the carnage. I snacked on a Twinkie and tried to figure out what I was going to do with the rest of my parent-free, rowdy, fun-filled teenage day.

You always see those movies where the parents leave the kids home alone and it always looks like a blast, right? Well, this was not one of those movies. It was pretty boring, to tell the truth. I just kind of hung out and eventually decided to go to bed early. Like, massively, embarrassingly early. But I figured I'd gotten such a lousy night's sleep the night before that I needed it.

Turns out, I was in for two lousy nights' sleep. Seriously, it was the same thing all over again, minus Mr. Boots with his foot in my nose. Same heavy chest feelings, same dampness, same weird feelings that I was being watched. Not pleasant, let me tell you. And this time there were no bones that I could blame it on.

I felt like I'd just fallen asleep when Tina shoved the cordless under my nose. I hadn't even heard it ring, but she had, and boy was she grouchy about it. She didn't say anything, she just chucked the phone onto my chest and left.

I picked up the phone and tried to make my voice work. "Wha?"

"Arlie, it's Ty. Look at the newspaper."

"Huh?" Words don't always make sense in the morning.

"The newspaper, Arlie. Look at it. We're in big trouble."

CHAPTER 6

DAILY NEWS

VANDALS DESTROY TWO PROPERTIES DOWNTOWN: KNOBLES TARGETED?

VANDALS ransacked and destroyed two downtown properties late last night, and authorities have no explanation as to their motives. Both KNOBLE'S PET EMPORIUM and KNOBLE'S HAPPY MART are near complete losses after the intruders destroyed inventory and damaged the buildings. Luckily, the Happy Hog escaped unscathed.

Authorities say that the intent of the break-ins was destruction and mayhem rather than robbery, leading them to believe that **AL AND SHEILA KNOBLE**, owners of both properties, may be the targets of some kind of personal vendetta. No suspects have been identified, and no organizations have claimed responsibility for the crimes.

I stopped reading. We'd been at the Emporium and the Happy Mart just yesterday and everything had been fine. It seemed like a pretty big coincidence that vandals had decided to hit the exact two places that Ty and I had gone. I tried to shrug it off, but I had a feeling that I knew exactly what both places looked like now—probably pretty much like our kitchen had yesterday.

I lunged for the phone to call Ty back, but it was ringing by the time I got to it.

"You read it?" Ty sounded just as caffeinated and nervous as I felt. "So what now, Arlie?"

"I think we'd better get our stories straight." Not

that we'd done anything wrong, but still, it never hurts to be prepared.

"Good plan. And now's the time for us to be good little criminals and return to the scene of the crime. Thirty minutes." Ty hung up before I could even answer, so I raced upstairs to get a quick shower. I figured by the scene of the crime that Ty meant the Happy Mart or the Emporium, but there was always the chance he meant the vacant lot where we'd found Cuddles. That's the problem with talking like you're on a TV show. Sometimes you don't really make any sense.

I decided on the Happy Mart and headed over to meet Ty, half afraid that showing up early was going to make me look guilty. But if Sheriff Shifflett was going to use that as a way of finding suspects, he was out of luck, because it looked like everybody in town had the same idea. Not that I should be surprised. This was the most excitement we'd seen all summer. Half the kids in our class were milling around trying to get a look inside the Happy Mart, even though it was cordoned off with that yellow police tape. It didn't matter, though—you could totally see inside, anyway. It wasn't hard. The door was gone. The only thing left was a big pile of wood shavings in the doorway. The Happy Hog was ankle deep in them.

Even though the street around the Happy Mart was packed to the gills with rubberneckers, it looked like the real excitement was going on down at the Emporium, so after a quick look around, I headed over there. Take the number of people at the Happy Mart, double it, and throw in an assortment of domestic animals and you can pretty much imagine what I found.

"Man, are we screwed or what?" Ty panted, running up to meet me. He looked around nervously. "We are so busted." A guinea pig scuttled over his shoe and hesitated like he was considering doing some serious climbing.

"We're fine, we've got alibis." I was going the positive route here. Although judging from the crime shows I've seen on TV, my alibi would never hold up in court. Heck, Mr. Boots couldn't even vouch for me.

"They're totally going to pin this on us, Arlie. Sheriff

Shifflett saw us at the Happy Mart. He knows we were at the Emporium, and he's already decided we're trouble. What's he going to think?"

I looked around to make sure nobody was listening in. That guinea pig was the only thing paying attention to us, and I didn't think he was going to squeal. But we needed to get it together fast because we were the shiftiest-looking people on the block. That clerk at Knoble's Olde-Tyme Ice Cream Shoppe had nothing on us.

"You were home, I was home. Shiflett saw us leave. Everything was fine when we left." The guinea pig lost interest in Ty's leg and headed over toward the town hall lawn.

"You know it was him, Arlie. And we led him there. It's our fault!" Ty hissed at me. I watched the guinea pig hop onto the lawn and start chowing down.

"Don't you get it? Our friend whose name starts with a C? It was him!" Ty hissed again. He was spitting and everything.

"Stop it, Ty. There's got to be some normal explanation here. We don't know it was Cuddles." I tried to clear my head and do a little rational thinking—not easy when you're still half asleep. Sure, Cuddles had been a terror when he was alive. But he was dead now. He was bones. And I wasn't quite ready to accept that some crazed undead hamster was roaming the streets causing chaos. Not yet, anyway. Call it denial.

I scanned the scene at the Emporium, trying to get an overview of the situation. Mr. and Mrs. Knoble were talking with some reporter, and Sheriff Shifflett was over by what used to be the huge plate-glass window, questioning Ricky. It was kind of disconcerting how huge chunks of the front wall of the Emporium were just gone now. And I thought our door was bad.

I spotted Carla Tate across the street holding a handful of something white, so I made my move. Carla's always been a great source of mine. Okay, she doesn't actually know she's a source. But she's always got the scoop, and if I bug her enough, she'll usually tell me things. I bounced over and gave her a big grin.

"Hey, Carla! Wow, pretty bad, huh? Wonder what happened?" I find that perky usually works in these situations.

Carla turned around and for the first time I got a good look at what she had in her hands. Gross me out, man. It was mice. Lots of them, squirming around like they were having some kind of huge mouse party.

"Hey, Arlie, grab that one there, okay?" Carla pointed her foot at a rat wandering by. It was acting all casual, like it was just out for a day on the town. "Do you mind? Before it gets away? We've got to rescue them."

I've got nothing against rats, but for some reason I was really not okay with the idea of disturbing this guy on his daily constitutional. And if you ask me, he didn't need rescuing—he was a rat who could totally take care of himself. But if there's one thing I've learned, it's that you make sacrifices in the course of an investigation. I scooped up the rat, who I instantly dubbed Mr. Sniffy for the way he waggled his whiskers at me and tried act like it was no big deal.

Carla didn't even seem to notice my sacrifice. "Poor guys, they're all over. Whoever trashed the place broke all the cages and let all the animals out. Looks like some kind of animal-rights thing, if you ask me."

"Really?" I was only half paying attention, I have to admit. Most of me was trying to figure out how I was going to ditch Mr. Sniffy without being too obvious about it. Since I'd picked him up, he'd pooped on my palm, dug his little claws into my hands, and was considering making a break for it. Up my arm. Which, I can guarantee you, is not an exit route.

"You think it was animal activists? Then why the Happy Mart? To confuse people?" Mr. Sniffy started to make his move, but those tiny claws on my wrist made me do an oh so attractive and uncontrollable spastic jerk that jolted him back down into my hand.

Carla nodded, pretending not to notice that I was having a spaz attack. "Probably, that makes sense." She dumped her handful of mice into a cardboard travel box and reached out for Mr. Sniffy. I handed him over gratefully and quickly brushed his little gifts onto the ground. "That way, it's not so obvious that it's them."

"I guess," I said. Sounded more realistic than Ty's theory, anyway. But then it didn't take much to sound more realistic than an undead hamster. Another rat wandered by and stopped to inspect my shoe. Time for me to make my escape. I am definitely a one-rat kind of girl.

Ty was over talking to Donna Cavillari and some brown-haired guy with his back to me. It looked like they were in charge of reptiles. I scooped up a passing ferret and headed over. I figured if my hands were full, I wouldn't get recruited for snake duty. It was great plan, and it would've worked perfectly if the ferret hadn't immediately freaked out and started trying to scramble up onto my shoulder like he was some kind of demented parrot wannabe. Maybe the snakes wouldn't have been so bad.

Ty saw me coming and gave a wave with the hand that wasn't holding a garter snake. "Hey, Arlie. Donna was just telling us how it's a mob thing."

Donna nodded and petted a small lizard she was

holding. "The Knobles are totally in with the Mafia, everybody knows that, right? This is payback," she said knowingly.

"Payback for what?" I wasn't seeing this one.

"Come on, Arlie, it's the mob. You make one wrong move, and that's it. Mr. Knoble? He must've done tons of things to tick them off."

Yeah, well, I could see that, actually. If I had violent tendencies, I might decide to target the Knobles. Heck, even if I didn't have violent tendencies. The knot in my stomach loosened a little. True or not, at least nobody was pointing fingers at me and Ty. And nobody had even mentioned the possibility that zombies or creatures of the night might be involved. That had to be a good sign, right?

"Hey, Arlie. So. How's Tina doing? She doing okay?"

Crud. I hadn't even paid attention to the brown-haired guy when I came over. Big mistake. I'd know that voice anywhere. I shifted the ferret and looked up at Trey Callahan, Tina's ex-boyfriend.

They broke up about a month ago, and he still didn't seem to be over it. At all. The most I can say is that at least he doesn't sit on our curb sobbing all night anymore. That really starts to get old after a while, let me tell you. Mrs. Murphy next door brought cookies out to cheer him up the first night, but it wasn't long before she was calling the cops and cursing in his direction. And when an eighty-seven-year-old woman is making a detour with her walker to curse at you, you know you're pretty irritating. It's not a good way to win someone back.

I'd been hoping that he was over her by now, but the pathetic quaver in his voice told me I'd better watch my step or we'd have our one-of-a-kind Trey Callahan lawn ornament back again.

"Tina? She's great! Fine. I mean, she's okay." Talk about awkward. I wasn't sure what tone to go with. I need to read more teen magazines. "Anything new with you, Trey?"

Trey's lip quivered, and the iguana he was holding slapped him on the mouth with its tiny green hand. It's pretty bad when even the iguana has heard enough.

"Where is Tina, Arlie? I'm surprised she's missing all the excitement." Donna smiled at me and patted her lizard again. A new one had appeared on her shoulder that I'm not sure she was aware of, but I didn't say anything. They were very well-behaved lizards. Better than Mr. Twisty the ferret. He'd given up on the climbing plan and was taking a healthy interest in my left nostril.

"She's at home training Mr. Boots—he's going to be in the talent competition. You know, *America's Most Talented Pets*?"

Donna nodded. "Good for her. You can never have too much training for that kind of thing. She's going up against Ted, you know. We've got high hopes."

"Oh really? That's . . . great." Man, the Jacobs family can not catch a break. Ted is Donna's supersmart and superhyper Jack Russell terrier. With Ted entering, Mr. Boots pretty much had no shot. I've seen Ted check the mail for Donna, turn on the house alarm when she leaves, and start her car using the keyless entry system. Most dogs just lift a leg to go to the bathroom, but Ted does a complete handstand and walks the length of the yard like he's auditioning for Cirque du Soleil. He's like a human in a dog suit. I don't think there's anything that dog can't do. Put it this way: If you dipped Ted's feet in paint and put him on a piece of paper, there'd be a bidding war at Sotheby's auction house for the result.

"So what's his talent?" At least I could give Tina the heads-up about the competition.

Donna shrugged. "Beats me. Whatever he feels like, I guess. He's really into yodeling now, so maybe that. We watched *Heidi*."

Great. Ted the yodeling canine acrobat. Mr. Boots was doomed.

"So does she ask about me ever?" Trey said through the iguana hand.

"What?" I couldn't believe he was still on that. I mean, okay, I could believe it, but sheesh, you know?

"Tina, does she . . . what I mean is, does she? Say anything?"

Maybe it was the ferret nose in my ear, maybe it was the whole Cuddles thing, or maybe I'd just had enough of Trey's whining, but I snapped. "Yeah, Trey, all the time, okay? You're all she talks about. Day and night, night and day, Trey Trey Trey." I knew as soon as I said it that I shouldn't have, but I couldn't help it. I mean, show some dignity, right?

Ted's eyes lit up like I'd stuck a candle up his butt. "Really?" he squeaked. The iguana slapped his other hand over Trey's mouth and swiveled his eye around to glare at me. There's nothing that makes you feel guiltier than an iguana shooting you a disapproving look.

I sighed. "No Trey, not really. She's over you. I think you should move on."

I turned to Ty and Donna for help, but they'd both gotten really interested in the sky and sidewalk respectively. And, unfortunately, for me, the help I was looking for came from the last person I wanted to see: Sheriff Shifflett.

"That's right, move on, son. I need to talk to Miss Jacobs and Mr. Parker here."

Sheriff Shifflett put one hand on my shoulder and one hand on Ty's shoulder and smiled at us. It was just a mouth smile though, not an eye smile, and not a very reassuring one either.

Trey just glared at the sheriff. For a second I thought he was going to say something stupid, but those little iguana hands seemed to be doing the trick of keeping him quiet, and he just trudged off after Donna. Trey thinks that Sheriff Shifflett is one of the reasons Tina broke up with him, and I don't think Tina said much to make him think otherwise. That just shows you how much brain power Trey has, if he thinks Tina would ever go for Sheriff Shifflett.

"Now you two want to tell me what you were doing here yesterday? Quite a coincidence, don't you think?"

I swallowed hard and tried to shift the ferret to a more comfortable position, but he was just twisting all over the place. Remind me never to get a ferret. It's like those things don't even have bones. He worked his paws into the hair at my neck and tried to burrow up into my head.

I ignored him and tried to act like I wear ferrets in my hair every day. "What do you mean? We were shopping."

"Same as you," said Ty. "We just wanted a Happy Dog."

"So you say." Sheriff Shifflett smiled again. "But it seems a mite suspicious, to my mind." He paused and stared at us until my eyes were watering, but we didn't crack.

"Well." Sheriff Shifflett broke the stare, thankfully. "So, while you were shopping. You see anything noteworthy? Anyone acting shifty, or hanging around the stores? Anything you want to tell me about?"

I tried to think if I'd seen anything I could mention, but I really couldn't. I would've loved to have had a suspect ready to throw at him, because I sure as heck wasn't going to mention Cuddles.

"No sir," Ty said, shaking his head. You know things are bad when Ty whips out the "sir" talk.

I shook my head too. "Nothing suspicious. Just you."

Sheriff Shifflett looked at us hard, like he was willing us to confess. Then he rolled his eyes. "Nothing, huh? Well, if you think of anything, you tell me. First thing. And I'll be keeping an eye on you two." He gave us a little push to send us on our way, which totally freaked my ferret out. I untangled it from my hair and dropped it down on the curb, where it streaked over to a tree and sat down to do some serious grooming.

"Now you two, git. Don't hang around here, that's loitering."

We nodded and took off. I was glad to see that the ferret had only gotten one paw done before Amber Vanderklander scooped it up. Serves it right for being so ornery.

Ty and I didn't say a word until we were two blocks away. Then Ty shook his head. "Man, Arlie. We're suspects."

"I know." I didn't know what we could do about it either.

"Well, only one thing to do now, am I right?" Ty draped his garter snake around his neck. I really think he should've given that back, but I wasn't going to say anything.

"Definitely. Time to see Mandy."

CHAPTER 7

MANDY'S HOUSE WASN'T WHAT I'D CALL HARD to find—I'm actually surprised me and Ty hadn't spotted it before and come by to gawk and take photos. It looked like an enormous pink cupcake sitting on top of the hill. Exactly the type of house somebody with unicorn-and-heart stationery would live in.

The outside was pink stucco that I would've sworn was that special bakery buttercream frosting, and it had fancy lacy trim all around the eaves and windows. The walkway had three lattice archways over it with vines and flowers growing all over them. There were hanging crystal fairies and reflective globes hanging on every branch, and the garden was filled with plaster statues of girls in prairie bonnets, garden gnomes, and whimsical animals in amusing poses. Well, amusing to them, I'm sure. As for me? Not that amused.

"Jackpot," Ty said, ducking out from behind a tree to check the mailbox and accidentally whacking his head against a wind chime in the process. Way to be discreet.

The mailbox was light blue and had curly calligraphy writing on the side. Burke-McGee. We were in business. I figured when we knocked on that door we had a fifty-fifty shot of getting either Mandy or Strawberry Shortcake.

We ditched our bikes in the bushes and started toward the walk. But as we got closer, it hit me how ridiculous this whole thing seemed. Having weird theories was one thing. Sharing them with a total stranger was completely different.

"Hold up, Ty," I said, grabbing the back of his shirt to keep him from trucking up the front walk. "Let's just take a minute? Make sure about what we're doing."

Ty rolled his eyes. "It's pretty obvious what we're doing, Arlie. Don't you think?"

Well, yeah, I did. But that was the problem. It didn't make sense.

"Let's look at the situation objectively, okay? Now. We're saying that Mandy's former hamster, Cuddles, has come back from the dead?"

Ty thought about it. "Pretty much."

"And we're saying that this undead hamster with an attitude problem has totally destroyed not only my kitchen, but two reputable businesses?"

Ty nodded. "You got it."

I sat down on the lawn. I figured if I hunched over, I might look enough like a prairie girl that no one would notice me. Besides, after two nights of Cuddles, I had the energy level of an earthworm. "That's what we're really saying? That we're cursed by a crazed undead hamster bent on destruction? And we're going to ask his former owner what to do about it?"

"Well . . ." Ty hesitated. "He's a big hamster." He groaned and sat down next to me. "Okay, we sound like crazy people. But what else could it be? Are we missing something?"

I fiddled with the wings on a dancing fairy and tried to be logical. But no matter how I thought about it, I kept coming to one conclusion: Cuddles.

"That's all I got. Dead hamster." Book my room at the loony bin now.

"Me too. So we're crazy people. Let's go with what we're good at. Crazy talk." Ty sighed and heaved himself up. "Heck, Mandy's the one who did the curse. Maybe she'll end up being crazier than both of us."

That was definitely a possibility.

"Okay. But let's try to act normal until we know for sure."

"Done." Ty gave me a hand up, and I brushed off my butt as we walked up to the house. I was going to try to be the sanest crazy person I could be. I took a deep breath and rang the doorbell.

Tinkly fairy chimes rang out all around us, but nobody came to the door. I figured they had to hear them—those chimes may have sounded pretty, but boy, would they get on your nerves after a while. We were just starting to fidget and feel weird about standing there any longer when a head peeped around the corner. It was a girl, and she was wearing a furry pink cat-ear headband. Not your usual look, but okay.

"Hey," I started, but the girl squealed and clapped happily before I could say anything else. It kind of freaked me out, to tell the truth. She had a really floppy stuffed cat hooked under one arm, which swayed when she clapped.

"Perfect! You guys will be great fairies. Come on!" She disappeared around the corner of the house.

Me and Ty exchanged worried glances. Nobody had ever told me I'd be a great fairy before, and I really wasn't sure how to take it. Compliment? This was really not how I imagined the day playing out.

Ty shrugged and headed off around the side of the house. I was only a couple of steps behind him, but by the time I got into the backyard, Ty was already wearing a pair of sparkly green deelyboppers on his head. I stifled a snort. Ty's tried a bunch of different looks over the years, but I never imagined him as part of the deelybopper crowd.

"That's a good look for you," I snickered. Great move, Arlie. Draw attention to yourself when there's a crazy girl three paces away wielding a pair of hot pink fairy wings.

The girl saw me and squealed again. "These will be great on you!" She danced over and started putting the wing straps over my arms. This had to be Mandy. The fairy routine, the headband, the pink unicorn shirt—they all just screamed heart-and-ribbon stationery.

It's a good look, maybe if you're six. But it's not like she was a little kid—she had to be a couple of years older than us, probably Tina's age, definitely a high schooler. I didn't recognize her, though, which I thought was weird, because I thought I knew everybody. And this girl definitely would've caught my attention.

"So who are you guys, anyway?" Mandy said as she fluffed up my fairy wings.

"We were just looking for Mandy. Are you Mandy?" I tried not to catch Ty's eye. Those deelyboppers were going to push me over the edge.

"That's me! I'm just working on a painting. It's of fairies, but I didn't have any, so you guys are perfect! I thought poor Puffkins was going to have to do all the posing himself."

I looked around, but I couldn't spot a Puffkins anywhere, unless she was talking about the cat stuffy that she'd draped over the table. I was starting to have serious doubts about this whole plan. It looked like the bus to crazytown had been here and Mandy had a reserved seat. I figured to heck with normal. I had a new plan—it was called get the heck out of Dodge.

"We can't really pose for a painting, Mandy. Sorry about that. No time." No wonder Cuddles was crazy.

Ty shot me a nasty look. "Hey, this is a weird question, but did you put a curse on your hamster?"

I couldn't believe it. Way to be subtle, Ty. Way to act sane, Ty. Way to ease into the topic. But Mandy didn't seem thrown by the question at all. She just giggled and started putting some green fairy wings on Ty.

"You mean Cuddles? Yeah, I guess I did. But not on him, just on his bones. He was dead when I did that. I don't even have hamsters anymore. Pretty silly, huh?"

Yeah, it was a real laugh riot. "Why'd you do that?" I said, probably a little more grouchily than I meant to. "That's kind of uncool, going around cursing things."

Mandy shrugged. "Oh, come on, it was just for fun. Here, you can pose with Puffkins." She scooped the cat stuffy off the table and held it out to me. She smiled and looked encouraging. "Don't worry, he's nice. He's not like Cuddles. He won't bite."

Yeah, no kidding, stuffed animals usually don't. But then Puffkins blinked. He wasn't a stuffed animal. He was a real cat and he looked grouchy as hell. He was just hanging there, legs completely limp and floppy, like he was doing some kind of limpness Presidential Fitness Test in gym or something. And he was staring at me like he was daring me to start something. But believe me, I know better than to pick fights with Mandy Burke's pets. I tentatively hooked my hands under his arms and grabbed him.

"This is going to be so great!" Mandy patted Ol' Floppy Legs and put a filmy scarf around his neck. "You and Puffkins make a cute couple. Now, who are you again? And what do you care about Cuddles?"

Ty cleared his throat and tried not to look at me. I had a feeling I looked as goofy as he did. "They're digging up the vacant lot to make the community pool, and we found Cuddles's bones with the curse."

Mandy adjusted Ty's wings and pushed him in front of a rose trellis. "So?"

"Well, since we found it, you know . . . we read the note. Nobody likes to be cursed!" Ty gave a forced laugh.

Mandy laughed too. "Oh, come on. It was just for fun. You know, like Egyptian tombs? And I didn't want my stupid brother Sam messing with his grave. Why do you think I buried him so far away? He hated that hamster."

"Really?" I decided to play innocent. "Why would he hate a hamster?"

"Man, who didn't hate Cuddles?" Mandy pushed me a little closer to Ty and arranged some garden gnomes around our feet. "Everybody hated him! But that's okay—he hated them worse. My mom always called Cuddles a nasty piece of work."

Ty winked at me. We were going the ignorant route. "What did he do? Did he squeak his wheel?"

"Cuddles didn't even have wheel privileges anymore after the first couple of weeks. He used to have one, but he kept waking everybody up. Only he wasn't running in his wheel, he was taking it apart and slamming it against the side of his cage. He got out that way once—completely shattered one wall of the aquarium and took off. We didn't find him for a week, and that was only after he chewed up the basement sofa and jumped onto Sam's face while he was sleeping." Mandy snorted. "Sam says he was trying to kill him, but he always exaggerates."

Ty gave me a significant look. He had a piece of green glitter on his nose. I averted my eyes and bit my lip. "So Sam thought Cuddles was a killer."

Mandy gave an exasperated sigh. "Cuddles wouldn't have really killed him—he was just into biting and chewing things up. Everybody in my family has scars, except for me. He never bit me, not once. Me and Poppy, my girl hamster, he liked us best. He was real sweet to me. He'd offer me sunflower seeds and everything. He was always bringing me little presents. That's why I wanted to make sure he had a good grave. Especially the way he died." Mandy frowned and squinted at us. "Could you maybe act like you're flying? Just lift your arms or something?"

"What happened?" I lifted one arm like I was flying, and tried to keep Puffkins from slipping out of the crook of my other arm. I'm serious, if I hadn't seen him blink, I'd swear he was dead.

"It was no big deal. Cuddles, he hated country music, okay? Couldn't stand it. And my family, we all like it. I mean, it's a big thing with us. Especially the Oak Ridge Boys, and Cuddles hated them most of all. So I was in the kitchen giving Cuddles a bath in the sink, right? And Sam, that idiot, he goes into the living room and starts playing 'Elvira' by the Oak Ridge Boys full blast. I mean, what did he think?"

"That's crazy," Ty said, shaking his head. His deely-boppers went wild. I'm serious, I think he was trying to crack me up. I bit my tongue and tried to think sad thoughts.

"That's what I said! Cuddles, he goes insane. He jumps out of the sink, does a bellyflop onto the dog bed, and starts a rampage in the living room. I'm not even sure what happened exactly, but he ended up knocking a lamp over into the dog dish, and then he must've run right through it. . . ."

"He was electrocuted?" Ty asked.

Mandy nodded. "It was really sad." She turned her back to us and started messing with something on the table. I felt like a real jerk, dragging this all up again.

"It all worked out for the best, though." Mandy turned around, camera in hand. She'd perked right up again. "Puffkins is a much better poser than Cuddles ever was. He always messed up his costumes. Say cheese!"

She snapped a picture of me, Ty, and Puffkins, which, I'm serious, had better not ever end up on the Internet or I'm suing. "I can paint from this."

I handed Puffkins back to Mandy, maybe a tad too eagerly. Puffkins totally creeped me out. It's like he'd totally lost the will to live. Living with Mandy will probably do that.

"Boy, that Cuddles," I said. "Sounds like a real nightmare. Too bad about the whole electrocution thing, though."

"Yeah, thanks. The house is a lot calmer with him gone, it's true."

I looked at Puffkins lying motionless on the chair where Mandy had put him. "I'll bet."

"Mom says my stepdad probably wouldn't have proposed if Cuddles had still been alive. Cuddles always attacked his ankles when he came for dinner."

Ty took off his deelyboppers and handed them to Mandy. "Yeah, whew! Cuddles sounds like the kind of hamster who could, I don't know, maybe totally destroy a store, right? Or chew down a door? Really wreck a place?"

Mandy stopped and just stared at Ty.

Ty gave me a nervous look. "Trash a kitchen, maybe? Right?"

Mandy snorted. "Yeah, uh, totally not what I said. He was a hamster, okay? Sure, he messed up the furniture and was mean and all, but hello? Hamster. Destroy a store? Sheesh. You guys are weird."

I think when the world's craziest elf girl calls you weird, that's your cue to leave. I was out of those wings so fast, they practically flew back to the table themselves.

Mandy punched Ty on the arm as we were leaving. "You guys are worse than Sam. I promise, you're not really cursed, okay?" She waggled the camera around in her hand. "Come back later and I'll show you the final product!"

"Sure, sounds good!" I chirped. Yeah, if I need an extra dose of crazy some week. No problem.

We headed back to our bikes, but Ty grabbed my handlebars before we left.

"I still think it's true, okay? I still think it's Cuddles."

I nodded. "Sure thing, Ty. Only problem is that his own owner says it wasn't. You heard Mandy. Sure, she's a psycho crazy chick, but she didn't curse us! It's all in our heads!"

Ty shook his head. "I don't know. Maybe. Let's check out the kitchen again. Maybe we missed a clue."

I nodded and we headed back to my house. Tina was on the phone in the kitchen, and judging from the way she was shrieking, it wasn't a good time to look for clues. We hightailed it upstairs to wait her out. I figured it was only a matter of time before she stormed upstairs and slammed her door.

We headed into my room and I flopped down on my bed. "So, what do we think is up? Someone really is after the Knobles? And they wanted Cuddles's bones, for some reason?"

Ty was looking at the floor at the foot of my bed with a weird expression on his face. This wasn't the time for him to lose it. I didn't think I could figure this out on my own.

"Hello, Earth to Ty?"

Ty looked at me. "What was it Mandy said about Cuddles? That he left her presents?"

"That was one of the saner things she said. Why?"

"You better see this." Ty pointed at the floor. I peered over the edge of the bed. The entire floor was covered with pet stuff—sunflower seeds, wooden hamster chew toys, rolling balls, and colorful bells.

Ty picked up a wooden chew toy and held it up. "I think you've got an admirer."

CHAPTER 8

IF SOMEONE HAD TOLD ME A WEEK AGO THAT a couple of sunflower seeds would make me recoil in horror, I would've given them a hearty smile and then backed away slowly. That's my standard operating procedure with crazy people. But the stash at the foot of my bed had turned me into the instant psycho, which I immediately demonstrated with a gale of gurgly hysterical laughter. Ty turned two shades paler. I'm not surprised—I sounded like I was practicing for a banshee-wailing competition. Heck, I scared myself.

"Funny joke, Ty." Man, it didn't even sound like my voice. "Funny, ha-ha. Stop now."

"Holy crap, Arlie. Cuddles is totally into you." Ty's eyes were wider than I'd ever seen them.

"Shut up, Ty. Not funny. Stop now."

"It's like he's got a major crush. Holy crap, Arlie! A dead hamster totally likes you."

"Not helping, Ty." I felt like my feet had taken root in the floor. Cuddles was skipping the getting to know you phase and had just moved right into my room. How the heck was I supposed to sleep there now?

"I mean LIKE like, Arlie. Not just like."

"I know what you mean, Ty!" This was definitely outside my range of experience. I'm not even sure how you're supposed to break up with humans. How the heck to you give a dead hamster the brush-off?

I looked at the little blue toy that Ty was holding. It was brand new. It still had the price tag and everything.

I stared at that tiny yellow tag and I felt like I was

going to puke. "Oh no, Ty. I am so dead."

Ty put a hand on my shoulder. "It's okay, Arlie. We'll figure something out. He's got to know it would never work out between you."

"Yeah, okay, that's a problem, yes. But I have a bigger problem. That toy is from the Pet Emporium."

Ty stared at the toy for a second and then dropped to his knees and started digging through the pile on the floor. "Oh, man. You're right. These are all new. And they all have Pet Emporium tags."

If I had any doubts left that Cuddles was behind the vandalism downtown, this pretty much killed them. Chopped them into tiny pieces with a huge sharp ax and then put them in the blender.

"My floor is covered with stolen goods. I'm in possession of hot hamster toys." I sunk down onto the ground and put my head in my hands. "My floor is covered with evidence."

Ty tried to whistle, but he still hadn't mastered the technique. At some point he needs to realize that it's just not going to happen for him. "If Shifflett sees this, you're going to juvie for sure."

"Me? What do you mean me?" I stared at Ty. "Don't you mean us?"

Ty stood up. "Well, not really. I mean, there's nothing to connect me with this. It's your room, your stuff. I'll stick up for you, but if Shifflett thinks you went all psycho on the Knobles, there's not a lot I can do. Besides, you don't want Cuddles bringing us both down, do you?"

Well, yeah, actually. I fiddled with a sunflower seed and tried to calm down. Panicking wouldn't help anything. Yeah, it was bad. But only if Shifflett found out.

I'd figure out a way to deal with Cuddles. And sure, wiping that smug look off Ty's face would be satisfying right now, but it really wouldn't help in the long run. I just had to make sure me and Ty were the only ones who knew about Cuddles's stash.

Of course, that's when the door flew open. I sucked in my breath so fast, I almost levitated a sunflower seed.

So much for keeping things quiet. It was Tina.

"Okay, Arlie, you have to go to the movie theater for me. And I mean now." Tina had Mr. Boots tucked under her arm like a football. "Get up, come on, hustle."

"Wha—?" I just stared. When you're in the middle of your own crisis, it's hard to suddenly switch gears and hop into someone else's.

Tina scowled at me and opened her mouth to give me a verbal smackdown, but that's when she caught sight of the loot at the foot of my bed. Chalk another one up for Cuddles—that was twice he'd managed to completely dumbfound Tina. Heck, and that was without trying.

"What the hell did you do, Arlie? What's all this stuff? Are those seeds?"

She kicked a little of the sunflower pile with her toe. So much for keeping the goods under wraps.

"Crafts," Ty said seriously. "It's a crafts project. And it's secret. A big secret. You can't talk about it."

"A secret crafts project. What, is this for your nonexistent summer school class?" Tina gave me a look that said she wasn't buying it for one second, but I was too drained to even care.

"Ty doesn't want people to know, okay? It's not macho to do crafts."

"Yeah, that's it." Ty glared at me. "I want people to think I'm macho."

Tina weighed this for a second and I guess she agreed with our premise that crafts equals not macho. She rolled her eyes. "Well, your crafts will have to wait. You need to get down to the movie theater and get Mr. Boots registered for the auditions." She shifted Mr. Boots, but apparently I didn't leap into action quickly enough, because she started to wig. "They don't take walk-ins, Arlie! Thank God I found out in time. We need to move on this!"

She went in for the pass, and suddenly Mr. Pigskin was under my arm, his little eyes bulging in terror. I could tell it had been a rough couple of days. All of his former cockiness had completely disappeared. I had a feeling that if you gave Mr. Boots a choice between a tasteful gingham ensemble and another afternoon of tap dancing, he'd go for the gingham in a heartbeat.

"Okay, but I've got a situation here, Tina. Can't you do it? Or can I go later?"

Tina cocked her head at me. "A crafts situation? What kind of crafts situation could you possibly have? No, I don't think so, Arlie. I need time alone to plan, or Mr. Boots is going to be a disaster on that stage. The dog can't play dead, Arlie. He can't tap dance, he can't walk a high wire, and he can't even juggle, for God's sake. Now get him out of here and get him registered while I think, okay? They close registration in an hour."

"Fine." Now that I thought about it, a little time away from Cuddles central would be really good. If I played my cards right, maybe me and Mr. Boots could get some fake passports and be on the next boat to Tahiti before anyone noticed.

I shifted Mr. Boots, who was curling up in a doggie fetal position, and decided that since I was on my way out, anyway, this was the perfect time to break the news about Mr. Boots's competition. I cleared my throat. "I ran into Donna earlier—she said she's entering Ted." I cringed and braced myself for the fallout.

Tina froze and gave me a cool appraising look. Not what I'd expected, but definitely better than an explosion. "Oh, really. Ted. How interesting. And what is Ted proposing to do for a talent?"

I shrugged. "She wasn't sure. She said maybe yodel. He saw *Heidi*."

Tina's face got bright red, and but still no fireworks. Instead, she got a strange expression on her face, kind of like the look you get when you're expecting to eat a piece of chocolate and you get a lemon Starburst instead.

"Hmm. Yodeling. Really." Tina stared at Mr. Boots. "Well, he's going to lose. Go sign Mr. Boots up, Arlie. I've got a plan."

She grabbed me and shoved me toward the door. Ty had to scramble to keep up.

"But what do I say if they want to know his talent?" I stammered. I was moving about three times as fast as

I would've been able to without my helpful Tina propulsion system, but still, it's never nice to be physically moved somewhere.

"Make something up. It doesn't matter. All that matters is that he's registered. They won't care what the form says when he wows them all." Tina shoved the Flexi leash into my hands, pushed us outside, and shut the door firmly in my face.

"Well. Guess we're going to register Mr. Boots." I snapped the Flexi leash on and put Mr. Boots onto the sidewalk. He promptly fell over on his side and rolled up like a pillbug. This struck me as a bad sign, talent show wise. I went the tough-love route and dragged him along until he got tired of bouncing and decided to use his feet.

"So, about Cuddles . . . ," Ty started.

I shook my head violently at him. "Ty, I don't want to hear it. I don't want to think about it. I've managed to get cursed, pick up an undead rodent stalker, and become a criminal accomplice. Some things you don't want to dwell on, you know?"

Ty nodded carefully, watching me like I tend to watch Tina to see if she's going to blow. It was kind of interesting to be on the other side for a change. Apparently no-sleep Arlie has a short fuse. "Arlie, I know. But you can't just ignore—"

"Forget it, Ty. See this doggie?" I grabbed Mr. Boots and jiggled him up and down until he started making gurgly noises. "This is Mr. Boots. It's his time right now. We don't talk about Cuddles when we're having Mr. Boots time."

Ty nodded. "Ooo-kay. No problem."

"Good. Just so that's clear." I put Mr. Boots back onto the ground, and he promptly did his pillbug routine again. I was beginning to think this might be a good talent for him. I bet none of the other dogs do pillbug impressions.

Mr. Boots decided to walk on his own again before we got to the end of the block, and we headed to Knoble's Cinema Palace in silence. When you've agreed not to talk about your huge, undead hamster problem, it pretty much turns into the only thing you can think about. It's not like we could make small talk about fairy pictures or unicorns or anything. But when we pushed open the doors to Knoble's Cinema Palace, what we saw immediately drove all thoughts of Cuddles away with a cattle prod.

I have to say, I've never been a huge fan of the show *America's Most Talented Pets*. Sure, the pets are cute, and their owners seem nice enough, but I can't stand the hosts, Tucker Tannon and Misty Morgan. First off, those can't be their real names—they seriously sound like the names of Barbie's friends, or flavored lip gloss, or maybe drinks with umbrellas. And on top of that, they look like mannequins come to life, with perfect supersprayed hair, gigantic Chiclet teeth, and big fakey smiles. In my opinion no one who smiles that much is up to any good. So you can pretty much imagine my feelings when I walked into a lobby that looked like someone had thrown up Tucker Tannon and Misty Morgan all over the walls.

A giant banner featuring Misty and Tucker and some

huge fluffy white dog was draped across the whole back wall. Every blank space was covered with posters of the hosts with various assorted animals. And scattered around the room were these freaky cardboard standees of them both, with arms that waved like they could see you. Personally, I think less is more when it comes to standees. At least stick to one per person—this place looked like someone had cloned an evil invading army of Misty Morgans and Tucker Tannons and they were using the movie theater as their base of attack.

Ty didn't seem to have a problem with any of it, though, or if he did, he didn't show it. He pointed at one of the smiling Tucker Tannon standees. "Hey look, it moves and everything. Cool." I even saw him waving back to a couple of them.

Obviously Ty's hell looks different from mine.

Amber Vanderklander was sitting at the table with a smug look on her face. I wasn't surprised to see her there—she's one of the popular kids at school, and she usually manages to make herself an essential part of whatever's happening. Working behind the scenes at *America's Most Talented Pets* is probably a gig that's pretty hard to get. It looked like the official-looking woman she was sitting with was letting her run the show too.

I headed over to the table, hoping Mr. Boots would look a little more impressive by the time we got there. One look at the standees and he'd gone into his pillbug routine again. I was hoping this wasn't going to be a new thing with him. I think I preferred Mr. Boots: Pervy Playmate Edition.

I went up to the table and smiled my best smile. "Hey, Amber! I'm here to register. Well, not me—Mr. Boots. What do we need to do?" I held up Mr. Boots and let him wow them with his cuteness.

Amber looked at her watch significantly. "Cutting it close, aren't you, Arlie? You're lucky we're still here. You need to fill out these forms. When you bring them back, tell us his talent and we'll assign you a time."

I put Mr. Boots down on the table so I could pick up the clipboard with the forms, and he toppled over again.

Amber poked him with her pencil eraser. "Is he okay?"

I laughed nervously and scooped him up with my free hand. He ended up dangling almost upside down, and the worst thing is that he didn't even seem to notice.

The woman on Amber's left patted her perm and gave a breathy snort. "Looks like that cat that was in here earlier. All the animals in this place that lively?"

"This is Mr. Boots, Beulah. He's kind of a local hero." Amber gave me an apologetic look. "This girl was here earlier and her cat looked seriously dead. Mandy something? I think she's a homeschooler?"

I nodded. "I know Mandy. Unicorn shirt?"

"Oh, yeah. That's the one."

"Great." So Mandy and Puffkins were going to be competing too. Good to know. Although I have to say, I wasn't that worried about whatever Puffkins might come up with. Does breathing count as a talent?

I took a quick look at the form. Thankfully it looked pretty basic. Filling it out wasn't going to be a problem. I figured I'd take my time, though. The longer it took to fill out the form, the more time I'd have to figure out what the heck to say Mr. Boots's talent was. What with looking at the clipboard, balancing Mr. Boots, and trying to come up with a talent, I didn't watch where I was going. Which is why I walked right into the person behind me.

"Hey, Arlie. Where's Tina? I thought Tina would be here. Didn't you say that?"

Oh, great. I looked up. "Hey, Trey. She's at home."

"Home? But I thought . . ." Trey visibly deflated. "Yeah, sure. No problem. I wasn't looking for her or anything. I could care less if she's here. I just figured, you know. Thought I'd come by."

"You don't have a pet," Ty said. Ty can be brutal sometimes.

"Well, but I'm thinking of getting one. Maybe a big dog. Or a cat. You know, a fluffy one."

I nodded. "Sure, Trey. Sounds good." I could see Trey years from now, living alone with a house full of fluffy cats and big dogs and pictures of Tina on every wall.

"So, she coming later, you think?"

"No, Trey. She's not coming, okay? Hey! Amber's nice, don't you think?" Okay, so I was desperate. If I thought it would get him out of our hair, I'd set him up with Mr. Boots.

Trey didn't look convinced. "I guess."

"Good! Why don't you guys talk? Maybe she can suggest a pet. Now, excuse me." I ducked behind a standee of Tucker and Misty playing with a dancing squirrel and settled down to work on the form. Like I expected, it took practically no time, but I kept hanging out behind the squirrel, anyway. It was nice to just sit and rest for a while. Besides, Mr. Boots was enjoying sniffing the squirrel's cardboard butt and I hated to disturb him. It was the first thing he'd seemed to enjoy in days.

"What are you going to say his talent is? Butt sniffing?" Ty looked at Mr. Boots skeptically.

"Don't forget, this is the amazing Mr. Boots. Hero of the Junior-Senior Prom. He's a celebrity, right? He doesn't have to do anything but look pretty." I hoped so, anyway.

"So that's his talent? Looking pretty?" Ty snorted. It wasn't an attractive display. Mr. Boots stopped sniffing and looked offended.

I sighed. "I don't know. Fetch or something? I could always put that he does impressions. He does a mean pillbug already."

Ty looked doubtful. Okay, so I'd better come up with a plan B.

"I don't know, then. Let's just get out of here. I need to go home, anyway. I've got to find a new place to sleep."

Ty nodded sympathetically. "Yeah. There's got to be someplace Cuddles won't go."

"I hope." I dragged Mr. Boots away from his squirrel friend and headed back over to Amber.

"All done with the forms?" Amber chirped, taking the clipboard and checking it. "Wait, you filled this out as Tina? Why'd you do that?"

Just my luck that Amber would be the one checking. That chain-smoker in the next chair never would've

128

noticed. "Well, he's her dog. I'm just registering him as a favor."

Amber hesitated, and then waved her hand. "Okay then, whatever. What's Mr. Boots going to do for his talent?"

"He's going to . . ." I had hoped that when they asked, some incredibly clever answer would just spring to my lips, but somehow it didn't quite work that way. Instead, I just stared at Amber like my brain had short-circuited.

"Come on, girlie, we don't have all day," Beulah the perm lady said, lighting another cigarette. "What's the dog going to do?"

"I can't . . . I can't tell you," I said. "It's going to be a surprise."

"Surprise?" Amber frowned. "I don't think that's allowed." I didn't think smoking was allowed either, but I didn't say anything.

"We have to know what he's going to do," Beulah said, scowling at me. I don't think she was a member of the Mr. Boots fan club.

Ty leaned forward. "We would, but you know the press. Once they get hold of this . . . watch out! We need to keep this hush-hush, if you know what I mean."

The perm lady gave Amber a look that pretty much called us crazy. "The press?"

Amber shrugged. "Mr. Boots is in the paper a lot," she explained. "That does make some sense. That *Daily Squealer* reporter was snooping around."

"Exactly! If it got out, all the other dogs would steal his act. I need to keep it quiet for now." I looked around like I was afraid someone would overhear. It must've looked convincing, because Trey seemed to notice, and edged a little closer.

The perm lady sniffed and inspected her nails. "I suppose it won't matter. As long as it's nothing indecent." She eyed Mr. Boots suspiciously. It was almost like she knew about his tendency to flaunt his nudie bits.

"Definitely decent," I swore. I just hoped it would be.

"You're all set then! You'll be after . . . let's see."

Amber checked the list. "We'll put you right after Mandy. Sound good?"

"Great." Actually, it was perfect. After that feline dust mop finished cleaning the stage, almost anything Mr. Boots did would look terrific. Maybe he had a shot after all. "Oh, and Amber? I think Trey wants to say hi."

Amber froze and then slowly looked over at Trey. Even Beulah put out her cigarette and craned her neck to get a look at him. He was standing next to one of the Misty standees, rubbing his nose. Not his best moment. After a couple of seconds of flat-out staring, Trey's sixth sense must've kicked in because he looked over and gave an uncomfortable wave. Amber turned bright red and suddenly got really interested in her paperwork. Somehow I don't think it was a love connection.

Ty held it together until we got outside. "Man, Arlie, that was harsh! What did Amber ever do to you?"

I smirked at him. "You never know, they could really hit it off. And then he'd be out of our hair."

Ty made a face at me and stopped when we got to the corner. "I'm heading home. No offense, but your house gives me the creeps. You want to sleep over? My folks'll let you stay in the guest room."

I shook my head. "If Mrs. Knoble found out about that one, she'd have my head on a platter. Maybe he's moved on."

"Maybe." Ty tried to look hopeful, but neither one of us really thought it was true. That pile of stuff was pretty much the equivalent of a hamster suitcase. "Good luck with the talent, Mr. Boots. And definitely let me know if our friend makes another appearance."

I nodded as Ty headed off toward his house, and then me and Mr. Boots trudged home.

We peeked into the kitchen, but there was no sign of Tina or Cuddles. I decided to take that as a good sign. I took Mr. Boots' Flexi leash off and looked around.

"Tina?" It was weirdly quiet.

"In here." Tina's voice came from the living room.

I poked my head around the corner. Tina was sitting on the big squishy couch in front of the TV.

"I've figured it out, Arlie. See? Check this out."

I plopped down onto the cushions next to her and looked at the set. I was expecting some video of animal tricks, but instead it was one of the movies Tina had collected during her pioneer obsession of a couple of years ago. Not many people know that she had a pioneer phase, and I've been sworn to secrecy. But a lot of the outfits Mr. Boots used to wear were actually made from Tina's old prairie dresses. Don't ask.

"Remember this?" Tina said. She clicked the remote. "It's *Skylark*, remember that?"

I nodded. One of the *Sarah, Plain and Tall* movies with Glenn Close.

"You said yodeling and it all came back to me. Remember this scene? It took me forever to find. Watch." She clicked the remote, and the movie started again. In the movie, there's a drought, and in this scene they load up the cows to take them off the farm.

"There, did you hear that?" Tina looked excited.

Okay, this is the thing. The tiny part of the movie Tina played? No dialogue. Nothing.

I shot a quick look over at Tina. She didn't look like someone in the process of flipping out. "Play it again." Maybe if I stalled for time, she'd go normal again.

Tina rewound the tape and played it again. And this time I knew what she was talking about. And it was bad bad bad.

At the beginning of the scene, the cows are all hanging around waiting to be loaded up, and then it's like one of the cows suddenly decided to go for his SAG card. Because seriously, it sounds like one of the cows says the word "hungry," but in a cow kind of way, so it's like "HONgry."

"Did you hear that? He says it again. Listen."

She played it again. The cow walked around and then said, "HONgry."

I swear to God, it sounded like the cow was talking, which usually I would've thought was awesome. But I knew where this was headed, and I don't think I've ever heard Mr. Boots say real words, even to himself.

I cleared my throat. "You think Mr. Boots can say hungry?"

Tina scowled at me. "Don't be ridiculous. What kind of talent is that? Saying hungry. That's lame."

I gave a relieved laugh. Of course she didn't expect Mr. Boots to talk.

"I'll have him say 'I love you.'" That'll be awesome. That'll wow them." Tina hugged a cushion to her chest and smirked.

"Can Mr. Boots say 'I love you?'" I asked hesitantly. Mr. Boots has his affectionate moments, sure, but as far as I know, he's never been one for expressing his emotions verbally. If he could, I think there would be a whole hell of a lot of things he'd be saying, and "I love you" would be pretty far down the list.

Tina shook her head. "Not yet. But it's only a matter of time. Look, I've researched this, Arlie. Barbara Walters has gone on record saying her dog can say 'I love you.' I've read articles. There are dogs on the Internet that can say it. Mr. Boots has a couple of days—how hard can it be? It's three words. It'll be great."

I just nodded. There was no way I was going to rain on her parade, not when I was likely to get fried doing it. "Well, good luck."

"Thanks. We'll get started on basic vowel sounds after we eat." Tina grinned. "Mrs. Knoble left a big container of soup and groceries on the back step with a note saying she hoped I felt better soon. Did you tell her I had the plague or something? She just rang the doorbell and ran."

I nodded. What Tina didn't know wouldn't hurt her.

Mrs. Knoble may not be the nicest person, but her cook Suzette is terrific.

Tina didn't even mention the auditions again until we'd polished off Suzette's chocolate cookies. But when she started getting out the flash cards, I figured I'd better make my escape.

I headed up to my room and inspected the pile of sunflower seeds and toys. It didn't look like it had gotten any bigger, so at least that was something. I tried not to think about the Twinkies from the night before. I'd just been encouraging the rodent, and I hadn't even known it.

Next I did a through Cuddles search—under the bed, in the closet, under the dresser, all the likely spots—but except for the pile of loot, I didn't see any signs of undead hamster activity.

My original plan was to stash all of the stuff in a bag and hide it in the closet, but when it came down to it, I couldn't bring myself to touch it. In the end, all I did was slump onto the floor by my dresser, stare at the pile, and wish it would all go away. I figured if I stared long enough, eventually I would figure out what to do.

Apparently what I decided to do was fall asleep in the most uncomfortable position ever, because in the morning I woke up with a huge crick in my neck and Tina hissing into my face. She looked really mad—I'm talking fire-breathing-dragon mad, not the-phone-woke-me-up mad.

"What is it?" I stammered. I hated to think what Cuddles had done while I was asleep.

"Get up, Arlie," Tina said, jerking me to my feet. "Sheriff Shifflett is downstairs. He's got some questions for you."

CHAPTER 9

"I CAN'T GO DOWN THERE!" I HISSED AT TINA. I grabbed the edge of my dresser and hung on for dear life. I wasn't going down without a fight.

Tina set her mouth in a grim line and started methodically detaching my fingers from the dresser one by one. "Oh yes, you can, Arlie. I've had the pleasure of talking to Sheriff Shif-flett for half an hour now, all because you put my name on that stupid form yesterday. You go down there now, or I'm sending him up."

"NO!" I let go of the dresser. I didn't have any idea why Sheriff Shifflett cared that I'd filled Tina's name in on the pet form, and I thought it was pretty sucky of Amber to turn me in if it was illegal. She could've at least warned me. But there was no way I was letting Sheriff Shifflett into my room to see my collection of stolen hamster goods. "I'll go, okay? Just don't let him in here."

Tina looked at me like I'd gone insane. "What, are you worried about your secret crafts project? Like he'd care about that," she snorted, and then looked suspicious. "Why would he care about that?"

"It's secret! Secret crafts! I'm going downstairs now, see?" If Shifflett wanted to arrest me for improper form filling out, I was fine with that. The worst that could be would be what, fraud? I just hoped no one had tipped him off about the vandalism. I wouldn't put it past him to use the form as a ruse to get into the house.

I hurried over to the stairs, but Tina grabbed the back of my shirt and hauled me back. "Not so fast, Arlie. When you get done there, I'm going to want an explanation for this."

She dragged me by my collar to the bathroom and shoved me through the door.

It looked like Christmas had come early in the Jacobs household, because the bathroom was knee deep in fluffy whiteness. Every bit of toilet paper in the bathroom had been chewed into tiny shredded pieces. I think a couple of towels had gotten added into the mix too.

"What the hell did you do to all the toilet paper, Arlie? Is this a craft too? You're just lucky I had a box of Kleenex in my room," Tina hissed in my ear. "I'll expect an explanation when you get back."

She let go of my collar and I made my escape, shooting down the stairs three at a time. Sheriff Shifflett was sitting on the edge of Mom's most uncomfortable chair. He didn't look any happier than Tina, but as far as I knew, he'd had a morning free of toilet paper issues.

"Arlene. Have a seat. I've already been talking with your sister Tina."

I perched on the edge of the couch, which was a huge mistake, because it's not made for perching. It's made for sucking you in and holding you hostage in its squishy softness. I did the best I could to sit up straight and not get sucked in.

"This is about that form?" I figured I'd just lay my cards on the table and then plead ignorance and beg forgiveness. Maybe blink my eyes a lot and try to look cute. Please let it be about the form.

"Ah yes, the form. This is the form you're talking about?" He held it up for me to see. "The application for the pet talent show?"

"I guess so." Maybe it would've been smarter just to let him start. Now I'd jumped in and I still had no idea what was making him so cranky.

"This form places you at Knoble's Cinema Palace yesterday afternoon."

I didn't like the way that sounded, but I decided to go along with it. "That's right. But I only put Tina's name because I was registering Mr. Boots for her. Amber said it was okay. She didn't say it was illegal."

Sheriff Shifflett gave me one of his nasty smiles and

ignored my explanation completely. "And you were seen at Knoble's Happy Mart and Knoble's Pet Emporium the day before. I have to say, Arlene, it looks mighty suspicious. Almost like you were casing the stores. What do you have to say to that?"

Sheriff Shifflett stared at me like he expected me to say something, but I didn't have any clue how to defend myself. Yeah, it looked suspicious, okay? I realize that. I'm not an idiot. But as for a plausible way to explain Cuddles—that was still on my things-to-do list. Serves me right for procrastinating.

"I wasn't. I was shopping," I stammered unconvincingly.

"You were seen at three Knoble-owned locations just a few hours before each one was vandalized. And you're telling me you were just shopping? That you had nothing to do with it?"

So the movie theater had been vandalized too. Thanks a lot, Cuddles. I tried to think of something clever to say, but I couldn't make my brain work. I mean, listening to

Sheriff Shifflett, I was almost convinced I was guilty too. Just hand over the handcuffs, I'll slap them on myself.

Sheriff Shifflett looked disappointed in me, like he'd expected some snappy answer. "Now, I'll need to know your whereabouts for the past three nights."

"I was home. But I can't prove it or anything. I was in my room." This was not going well. I wondered if Ty would visit me in jail.

Sheriff Shifflett sighed. "Mrs. Knoble is watching you while your parents are out of town. Is that right?"

"Right."

"Do you have some sort of grudge against the Knobles, Arlene? Are you angry at them for some reason?"

"No! They're fine, okay? I don't hate them any more than I hate Mrs. Murphy next door!"

Shifflett's eyes narrowed. "You hate Mrs. Murphy next door?"

"No! I don't hate either of them!" I desperately started weighing my options. If I spilled the beans about Cuddles, they'd think I'd lost it, which would mean a mental ward. So jail, or a rubber room. I couldn't decide which would be better.

"So what you're saying is . . ." Sheriff Shifflett paused as Mr. Boots came prancing down the stairs, nails clicking like crazy, and planted himself at the foot of the stairs. I glanced over to see what had made Sheriff Shifflett stop talking. I should've known. Mr. Boots had gone informant. He had a sesame hamster treat in his mouth, with a yellow price tag blazing like a beacon from the end.

Mr. Boots waggled the treat around in his mouth and then ran off into the kitchen. I'm serious, that dog might as well have gotten his paints out and made a sign with a big arrow pointing upstairs that said EVIDENCE THIS WAY. Sheriff Shifflett leaned back in the chair and gave me a cool appraising look.

"So, looks like you picked up some items from the Pet Emporium. Mind if I take a look?"

"Sure, no problem!" I squeaked, trying not to hyperventilate. There was no way Sheriff Shifflett would believe that all that stuff had been in the bag I had with me at the Happy Mart.

Sheriff Shifflett got up and wiped his hands on his pants, but instead of heading up the stairs like I'd expected, he headed into the kitchen after Mr. Boots. Don't believe people who tell you not to play with your food—Mr. Boots's disgusting see-food display may have saved my butt.

I hustled into the kitchen just in time to see Sheriff Shifflett taking the remains of the sesame stick out of Mr. Boots's mouth. Mr. Boots didn't even complain, he just flopped over and exposed his belly. Way to defend your home turf, dog.

"This doesn't look like a dog treat, Arlene. You bought this at the Emporium? I suppose you have the receipt?"

"I guess, I mean—I don't know. . . ." Way to improvise, Arlie. Luckily my stammering was cut off when Sheriff Shifflett suddenly pushed past me.

"Whoa, Nelly, what's all this?"

Crud. I'd totally forgotten about the hole gnawed in our kitchen door. I need to start writing things down.

"What happened here, Arlene?" He crouched down and inspected the door. It still looked pretty bad. The cardboard I'd stapled on there didn't really do much to make it look better.

"That? Um. I'm not sure, really. It happened the other night. Right after my parents left."

Sheriff Shifflett looked up at me. "The night before the vandalisms downtown?"

"That's right. Tina thinks Mr. Boots did it."

Sheriff Shifflett gave a scary barking laugh that sent Mr. Boots heading for the hills. "That little dog couldn't make a dent like this. No, this took some serious doing. Someone try to break in here?"

I shrugged. Break *out* was more like it.

Sheriff Shifflett balanced on the balls of his feet and stared at me. "Quite a coincidence that Mrs. Knoble was responsible for you girls when this happened. Did you see anyone suspicious hanging around here that night?

Someone who might have a grudge against the Knobles? This could be connected."

Great, now if I got busted, it would be for vandalizing my own house. The Happy Mart, Mom could forgive, but her own kitchen? I was so dead.

"Couldn't it be something totally different? What if it isn't someone with a grudge against the Knobles? What if it just looks that way?" I blurted out, like I'd turned into some kind of erupting word volcano.

Sheriff Shifflett narrowed his eyes at me. "You mean a setup? You're thinking that's what someone wants it to look like?"

Well not quite, but sure, sounds good to me.

Sheriff Shifflett stood up and hooked his thumbs in his waistband. "Interesting theory. Now, Mrs. Knoble—did she know about this? She's seen this damage?"

I shrugged. "I guess so. She didn't say anything, though."

"And she didn't call the sheriff's office to report it. Interesting." Sheriff Shifflett brushed off his pant legs.

"Well, Arlene, thank you for you time. You've been very helpful here."

I could feel the knots in my neck start to loosen. No jail for Arlie, at least not today. And Shifflett was leaving. Maybe today wasn't going to be that bad after all.

He tapped the cardboard with his foot. "We've got to get this boarded up good and proper. This flimsy cardboard wouldn't keep a chipmunk out. I'll send a deputy along in a bit to fix things up for you. I'll have a car patrol this area to watch you girls too." He looked around the kitchen. "Hate to think what could've gone on here. And I promised your mother I'd keep an eye out. If you don't mind, I'm just going to take a quick look around inside before I go. Just to make sure everything's as it should be."

My stomach dropped like it was on a roller-coaster ride. "Well, okay, but we're fine. I mean, we've been fine. Nothing weird going on here. No, sir." I tried to laugh nonchalantly, but my psycho banshee wail seemed to have morning duty. Great.

Shifflett patted me on the shoulder awkwardly. "Just need to be sure. Got to keep you girls safe."

He checked all the closets and rooms downstairs and then headed upstairs. I tried to kick-start my brain to think of a plan. Once he saw that bathroom and the mess in my room, I'd be toast. I figured I had one shot left to save myself, and the only idea I could come up with was superlame.

When Sheriff Shifflett reached the top of the stairs, I shot in front of him and slammed my door shut.

"Sorry, that's just my room, and boy is it a mess. Nothing to see there."

Sheriff Shifflett nodded. "Seen messy rooms before, Arlie. Step aside, please."

"But, it's *super*messy. Not just messy. Dirty under-wear. Girl stuff. Female products."

Shifflett reached out, took me by the shoulders, and then picked me up and moved me two feet to the side. Like I was a puppy or a broom or something. I didn't even have time to be shocked.

Shifflett opened the door and stepped inside. After a couple of minutes, he came back out and shut it behind him.

"I've seen worse," he said, with a slight smile. Then he moved on down the hall.

I waited until he'd checked the hall closet and gone into Tina's room to open the door to my room. My bedroom floor was completely clean. No seeds, no shredded paper, no nothing. Everything was gone. It was like Cuddles's pile of goodies had never been there.

I sat down on the bed in shock. It barely even registered when Shifflett stuck his head in the door before he went back downstairs.

"Now you girls call if anything else happens. This isn't a joke, now. These are serious criminals we're talking about here."

I just nodded and did some more staring. I had almost convinced myself that the whole thing had been a horrible dream when Tina came in and dumped a huge trash bag on my floor. I didn't need to look inside to know what was in there.

"You owe me," she said. "Big-time. Now give it to me straight. Did you vandalize the Knobles's stores and take this stuff? Because it's cool if you did, I just want to know."

I shook my head. "I didn't take it."

Tina stared at me, waiting for more explanation, but that was all she was getting.

"Okay, question number two. Do you have a hamster or a gerbil stashed around here or something? Because this is all hamster stuff." She kicked at the bag. "And I am seriously not having a rodent in this house, okay?"

"I didn't buy a hamster." That wasn't technically a lie, right?

"Well, keep it that way." Tina scowled and grabbed at something under my bed. She came out with Mr. Boots by a leg. I hadn't even known the little guy was under there. She chucked him onto my bed, where he promptly burrowed under my pillow.

"And now? The answer to question number three?" Tina crossed her arms and tapped her foot.

"Question number three?"

"The bathroom? What the hell, Arlie? You use the bathroom too, you know. I'm not the only one who's got a problem with no toilet paper."

"Uh. Yeah. Sorry about that. I'll get some more." I figured, why even bother with an explanation? I seriously doubt Tina would believe that I sat up all night tearing the toilet paper into tiny pieces. And if she would believe it, I really didn't want to know.

Tina rolled her eyes at me and dug Mr. Boots out from under the pillow. "You better. And, Arlie? Get it together, okay? I just got QUESTIONED. By the SHERIFF. Not cool."

I nodded.

"Now, are you going to get the phone? I need to practice with Mr. Boots. He's so close now. Say it, Mr. Boots. Say 'I Love You.'"

I hadn't even heard the phone ringing, that's how out of it I was. Mr. Boots stared at me plaintively as I got up to go get the cordless.

"Say it, Mr. Boots. Use your words."

Mr. Boots looked anxiously from me to Tina, and then opened his mouth. "Arr?"

Poor guy. He was doomed.

I headed downstairs and grabbed the cordless. I didn't even need to ask who it was—I figured Ty was the only person who would let it ring and ring like that.

"Have you seen the paper?" Ty asked as soon as I said hello.

"Not yet. I was a little busy being questioned by the police."

"Well, go look. I'll wait."

I put down the phone and went for the paper. If Ty didn't even bother to ask what I meant about "the police," it must be pretty bad.

I grabbed the papers out of the mailbox holder and checked the headline.

DAILY NEWS

ANOTHER KNOBLE BUSINESS VANDALIZED
KNOBLE BLASTS SHIFFLETT: INCOMPETENT SHERIFF HAS NO LEADS

KNOBLE'S CINEMA PALACE was vandalized last night, making it the third business owned by local businessman AL KNOBLE to be vandalized in two days. Owner Al Knoble blasted SHERIFF BUCK SHIFFLETT, saying that the investigation into the vandalisms at his businesses has been mismanaged and mishandled.

In a press conference, Al Knoble said, "Sheriff Shifflett's incompetence has made it seem unlikely to me that these vandals will ever be caught. Shifflett himself was seen having a violent outburst at KNOBLE'S HAPPY MART just hours before the store was destroyed. Coincidence? Perhaps Shifflett himself should be a prime suspect. . . ."

I chucked the paper onto the table. Well, that explained why Sheriff Shifflett was so testy. I picked up the phone. "Got it. I know already, though—Sheriff Shifflett was here and told me about the movie theater. I'm totally a suspect."

Ty groaned. "No, Arlie, not that paper. The *Daily Squealer*. Check that one. Front page."

I put the phone back down and headed over to table, where I'd put down the other paper. Why Ty couldn't just tell me what was such a big deal, I had no idea. I think he liked the drama.

I picked up the *Daily Squealer* and it was pretty obvious what Ty was talking about. Right at the bottom of the front page there was a huge headline:

THE DAILY SQUEALER

MR. BOOTS'S MYSTERY TALENT: WHAT WILL EVERYONE'S FAVORITE CANINE DO FOR HIS TALENT?

MR. BOOTS, town hero and canine celebrity, has signed up to participate in auditions for AMERICA'S MOST TALENTED PETS. The town is abuzz with speculation—what does the multitalented pooch have planned? According to experts . . .

I stopped reading. There was even a sidebar article on Ted, talking about his yodeling prowess and how gutsy it was of him to try to take Mr. Boots's place in the hearts of the townspeople.

Not great news, sure, but it's not like the *Daily Squealer* wasn't constantly running Mr. Boots updates, anyway. This one wasn't any worse than the others.

I picked up the phone. "So it's out that Mr. Boots is auditioning. It's okay. I don't think Tina's going to care."

Ty sighed so hard, it sounded like a hurricane in my ear. Not a good feeling.

Obviously, I was missing something. "Okay, what?"

"Top of the page, Arlie. Look at the headline."

I turned the paper over. You know when people say

it feels like they have ice water in their veins? Yeah, that's the feeling I got. Because this headline was going to blow everything wide open.

THE DAILY SQUEALER

STRANGE GLOWING CREATURE SEEN IN VANDALIZED STORES COULD STRANGE VISITOR BE RESPONSIBLE FOR MAYHEM?

Witnesses say that the strange alien creature seen destroying three local businesses looked like some sort of huge, glowing rodent. . . .

"Oh crud, Ty. It's about Cuddles."

"Exactly."

"What are we going to do?" If the *Daily Squealer* was onto Cuddles, it was only a matter of time before they zoned in on me. Especially now that Sheriff Shifflett had seen the kitchen door.

"We've got to figure something out, and fast," Ty said.

Yeah, like that hadn't occurred to me. "Okay, cool. Look, I'm sick of this place—how about I come over to your house and we can strategize? See you in a minute." If we played our cards right, maybe Ty's mom would make some of her fancy caramel popcorn. Nothing says breakfast like caramel popcorn.

"NO!" Ty must've screamed into the phone because I was about to hang up, but I could hear him crystal clear. Heck, I think he made Mr. Boots jump a foot into the air, and that dog was upstairs with problems of his own. "Are you crazy, Arlie? You can't come over here!"

Well, no need to get cranky about it. "Okay, fine. Why don't we meet downtown, then? We could get ice cream." Nothing says breakfast like a big scoop of ice cream.

"Are you insane?" Ty was using the big voice again. It was hurting my ear. "You can't go ANYWHERE, Arlie. He's following you! Don't you get that?"

I sat down hard on one of the kitchen stools. This was not what I wanted to hear. "You think so?"

"Duh!" I could practically hear Ty rolling his eyes at me. "Your house is trashed. Every place you've gone since we found the bones has been trashed."

I went back over everything I'd done. "Not true! What about Mandy's? He didn't trash Mandy's house."

"You didn't go inside Mandy's house," Ty said. "Look—I've got a plan. You stay there. I'm coming over. I think Mandy is the key to this all. I'll come over and then we'll go talk to her. But you have to stay outside. Got it?"

I nodded miserably. As much as I hated to admit it, Ty was right. Just call me Typhoid Arlie.

"Ty?" I said in my most pathetic voice.

"What is it?"

"Can you bring toilet paper?"

CHAPTER 10

AFTER I GOT MYSELF CLEANED UP, I WENT OUT-
side and sat on the stoop to wait for Ty. Tina'd
gotten a call from Amber after I'd hung up, and
she was working on a serious bad mood. Word
on the street was that since the movie theater
was pretty much a lost cause, they'd moved the
auditions to the junior-senior high auditorium
and everybody was going to have to reregister.
Tina told me to go down to fill out the forms
again, but I begged off, saying I had a lot of
important stuff to do. Okay, not quite true—
but it wouldn't have sounded as good to say

that I ran upstairs and hid in the hall closet until I heard her leave the house. (And I only rested my eyes for a second, I swear.) Although I have to admit, I was tempted to go down there just to see what Cuddles would do to that auditorium.

It was only a couple of seconds before I saw Ty coming my way. And as promised, he was carrying a big plastic grocery bag filled with absorbent cottony softness. Unfortunately, it looked like I wasn't the only one on the lookout. As soon as Ty got to my house, Mrs. Knoble came shooting out of her house like a clicky high-heel-propelled bullet, a smug look on her face. She must've seen Tina leave. I was so busted.

"What did I tell you about having boys here, Arlene?" She folded her arms like she expected me to beg forgiveness.

"Sorry, Mrs. Knoble. Ty was just helping us out. You know—Tina."

Ty opened up the plastic bag and pulled out a jumbo pack of toilet paper. He'd gone all out too—it was the supersoft, fifty-ply stuff that bears seem to be so fond of. It was actually a little scary looking—seriously, I don't think we could use that much in a year.

Mrs. Knoble's eyes bulged a little. I don't even want to know what she was imagining. But I think it's safe to say she thought Tina was taking care of business inside the house. "Oh. I see. Well, remember, you can always come to me, Arlene. I would've gotten that for you. Now, I won't keep you. Let me go talk to my Suzette—I'll have her whip something up for you girls that will be easy on the stomach."

I tried for a sweet innocent smile. "That sounds great, Mrs. Knoble. Tina loved the soup."

Ty nodded. "Until . . . you know." He shrugged.

Mrs. Knoble's eyes got wider and she twisted her mouth around in what I took to be a smiley shape. Personally, I think Ty was being a little cruel, not to mention disgusting. Mrs. Knoble didn't need that image in her brain. Heck, neither did I.

"Well, must run! Suzette, you know," she said as

she clicked back into her house at warp speed.

I shook my head at Ty. "That was just mean. And, believe me, if Tina finds out, you'll be needing this toilet paper to wipe yourself off the floor." I opened the door and stashed the package inside.

"I'll risk it," Ty said, doing his scariest kung fu hand motion. Like Tina would be afraid of that.

"You're a rebel, Ty." Someday there's going to be a Tina-Ty deathmatch, and when it happens, I want a front-row seat. "Now what's this big plan of yours?"

"I'll tell you on the way," Ty said.

We grabbed our bikes and headed out toward Mandy's house.

Not the easiest way to have a conversation, but luckily it's mostly backroads out there, so we could weave all over without worrying about getting squashed.

"Remember how Mandy said that Cuddles only liked her and her girl hamster? That he hated everybody else?" Ty almost ran his bike into a telephone pole, but managed to do a fancy recovery by swerving into a drainage ditch.

"Yeah, so?"

"So we get that girl hamster. We bring it to your house, Cuddles falls in love, and then you give it back to Mandy. Or you donate it to the elementary school of something." Ty snickered. "That would be awesome. Cuddles at an elementary school?"

I had doubts about Ty's plan. I was starting to wish I'd done a little planning on my own instead of just relying on Ty's bright ideas. Because honestly? Not usually so bright. It's pathetic—give me a little toilet paper and I stop thinking straight.

"Ty, she said she didn't have hamsters anymore."

Ty snorted and almost wiped out on the gravel. "I bet she has at least one. Come on, that girl? She's probably got pets coming out of her ears."

Hard to argue with that. "But are you sure it'll work?"

Ty skidded his bike to a stop. "Arlie, no offense, but he's known you, what? A couple of days? This hamster girl was his lifelong friend. I'm sure he'd rather hang out with her than with you. I mean, come on, you're not THAT awesome."

I tried not to be offended. Being snubbed by an undead hamster friend is a good thing. It's what every girl dreams of, right?

We ditched our bikes in Mandy's bushes and headed around the house to find her. I had a feeling she'd be out there in her fairy wonderland, and sure enough, there she was. Puffkins was reclining on the back deck, dressed up like a pirate. I say reclining, but really—reclining, propped up, hard to tell. A couple of gigantic plastic seagulls were hanging over his head, and he had an old bottle labeled xxx next to him. It looked like some kind of drunken pirate cat sequel to *The Birds*.

Mandy had skipped the cat ears this time and instead had her hair curled up in Princess Leia buns. She seemed just as happy to see us, though.

"You're back!" she squealed, dancing over to us. She grabbed Ty by one arm and reached for me, but I managed a subtle sidestep that put me out of range. I'm not stupid. I saw the bandanna and eyepatch in her hand.

She didn't waste any time getting Ty all decked out like Bluebeard, either. "So you guys wanted to see the picture? Is that it? It came out really great." She grabbed a big black pirate hat emblazoned with a skull and crossbones off the table. "Here, put this on and I'll go get it." She plopped the hat on Ty's head.

"Uh, that's okay, Mandy. We actually . . . ," I started, but Mandy disappeared inside the house before I could finish. I gave a sidelong glance at Ty and snickered. "Pretty scary, Ty. Arrr."

"Shove it, Arlie," Ty said, looking around nervously. "She doesn't have the camera out here, does she? I don't want this recorded for posterity."

I glanced around, but I hadn't spotted one before Mandy came back out. She was carrying a big canvas in one hand and a fake parrot in the other. That parrot was the last straw—we had to get out of there.

She shoved the parrot into my hands and then propped up the painting. Ty and I both gasped. It was amazing.

Seriously, if I ever turn into a pig, I bet that's exactly what I'll look like. Because chances are pretty good that Pig-Arlie will also go completely insane, and then I'll have the same scary psycho look in my eye that the Pig-Arlie in the picture had. And I'm not kidding—total insanity is the only thing that will ever get me in that outfit again.

Ty didn't fare much better. He didn't look like a pig, though. He looked more like a weasel or squirrel being attacked by crazed mutant deelyboppers. The only one who came off well at all was Puffkins, and that's just because he looked more animated than he did in real life. Not like that's hard, though.

"Wow," Ty said.

"Yeah. Double wow," I said. Words failed me. I didn't think I could even go the "that's really interesting!" route on this one.

"I know, isn't it awesome? This one's going to be even better, though. Put on your parrot."

I shoved the parrot back into Mandy's hands. No way

was I getting involved in any pirate activities. "We can't. Actually, we just stopped by to see the picture and ask you something."

Ty took off his hat. "Yeah, that girl hamster you mentioned? Cuddles's friend?"

Mandy rolled her eyes. "Are you guys still on that Cuddles kick? Sheesh, give it a rest! Are you obsessed or something?"

"Hey, just curious, that's all." Ty had his shifty *I'm such a liar* look, but Mandy didn't seem to notice. "That girl hamster? You know who we're talking about, right? Cuddles liked her a lot?"

"Poppy? Yeah. He thought she was the greatest," Mandy said, reluctantly taking the hat back and smacking it down on the table. "So what about her?"

"So do you still have her? Can we see her?" I held my breath. This could fix everything. "I'm, uh . . . thinking of getting a hamster."

"Sure, she's over there," Mandy said, pointing.

Me and Ty both craned our necks to look, but I didn't

see anything that looked hamsterlike. "Where is she?" I tried not to sound too eager.

"Over there, next to the tree? That's where I bury all my pets. Well, except for Cuddles. Hers is the grave on the end. She has the big bumblebee marker with her name on it."

My insides turned to goo. Of course it had been too much to expect. I don't know why I seriously expected Poppy to still be alive, especially since hamsters live, what, ten minutes?

We all trooped dutifully over to the patch of graves under the tree by the road. It was like a tiny Arlington Cemetery, the graves were so neat and tidy, except I don't think the graves at Arlington are marked with smiling bumblebees and happy dancing frogs.

"Yeah, well, that's her," Mandy said, pointing at Poppy's little marker. "If you really are considering a hamster, though, I think you'll get a better idea about them at the pet store. Poppy's not anything like she used to be."

"Wow. That's sad," Ty said. "So she was a good hamster? Not like Cuddles?"

Mandy shot Ty a nasty look and whipped his eyepatch off. I could hear the elastic smack him and everything. It sounded like it was going to leave a mark. "Cuddles was good too, okay, but just in his own way. But, yeah, Poppy was a cutie. Real sweet."

"Man, such a loss," I said. Mandy shot me a suspicious look, but I tried to look ultra sincere. Like I knew what to say. Graveside sympathy has never been my thing.

"So how'd she die?" Ty asked, taking off the bandanna. I think he knew that Mandy would be going for it eventually, and wanted to protect his tender neck.

"Natural causes, I guess. I didn't do an autopsy or anything, though."

Boy, that Mandy was just a whole sack of loose screws. All I wanted to do was get the heck out of there—I don't know why Ty was insisting on dragging this whole thing out.

"Well, that's good, at least. Good luck with your pirate picture. It looks nice."

Mandy looked back at Puffkins, who hadn't moved a millimeter since we'd shown up. I like to think that he'd drifted into a coma about the time we got there. "Oh, that's not really for a picture. I mean, it could be, if you guys wanted to help, but we were just rehearsing. You know, for the auditions? Puffkins is trying out for *America's Most Talented Pets*."

Yup, Mr. Boots's chances were looking better all the time. "Really? My sister's dog is entering that too. Looks like it's going to be a tough competition."

Mandy nodded. "Yeah, I bet. We're still working on the routine, though. He's not definitely going to be a pirate. He probably won't be, actually." Mandy gave me a hard stare, like she thought I was trying to steal her ideas.

I figured my best bet was to play completely dumb. "Yeah, I don't even know what Mr. Boots is doing. I'm not really helping at all."

Mandy nodded, but her eyes were still boring into me. I can take a hint.

"Well, good luck. Gotta go, okay? 'Bye!" I grabbed Ty by the arm and dragged him back over to our bikes. "Man, is Mr. Boots going to kick butt or what? Ted's the big competition, and Mr. Boots can probably take him." Except for the fact that he hadn't actually learned his talent yet.

"Okay, Arlie? I've got it." Ty stopped dead still and put his most serious face on. "I know what to do with Poppy. It's actually perfect. Now just listen and don't freak out."

I propped my bike up and stared at him. "Did you miss the news flash, Ty? Poppy's dead. That plan is over."

Ty's eyes gleamed. "No, it's even better! Cuddles is dead, right? Well, so is Poppy! So what we do is, we dig Poppy up and bring her to your house. Then, when—"

"Whoa, hold it right there. We dig her up?" This whole scenario was just grossing the heck out of me.

"Yeah. So then, we bring her to—"

173

"Not yeah! No yeah here. We are not digging up Poppy's grave, Ty. Cuddles—sure, that was an accident. But I'm not a stinkin' grave robber, okay?"

"But, Arlie, this could work. Just listen?"

"Dig her up, and then what? Create a tiny Bride of Cuddles? I've seen those movies, Ty, and things don't go well."

Ty sighed in frustration. "This would be different, Arlie, because Cuddles loves Poppy already."

"Yeah, and so then what? They start having a whole brood of undead hamster babies in my bedroom? I don't know if you understood what I told you about our toilet paper situation? We cannot handle a houseful of undead hamster babies. We can't even handle one. So forget it. No way."

I got on my bike and rode off down the street.

Ty wasn't far behind me. "Come on, Arlie, just think about it! It makes sense!"

I decided not to dignify that with a response. Next thing you know, Ty was going to suggest we find a way to conjure up evil demons to come get Cuddles for us. No dice, buddy.

Ty zipped out in front of me, and then crossed his arms and rode no-hands in that show-offy way he has sometimes. "Sorry, Arlie. I didn't realize you were the jealous type."

I swerved in front of him and almost made him wipe out in a bush. It was only partly intentional—mostly I hit a gravel patch and lost control, but I tried to make it seem like I was being an edgy risk taker. "I'm not jealous, okay? I just don't want a whole brood under my bed."

"Arlie's jealous that her hamster boyfriend will find a new girl." Ty did a singsong variation of that idea the entire way home, sometimes emphasizing the hamster boyfriend part, sometimes emphasizing the jealous part. It was a really mature display, let me tell you.

He kept it up until we got onto my street, when we suddenly found ourselves smack in the middle of somebody else's very mature display. Tina and Trey's, that is.

"That's it, Trey! It's over! Get the hell off my lawn."

Tina was using her low warning voice, which usually came right before the massive explosion.

"I just happened to be there, I swear. I just love the kitties, Tina!" Trey was practically groveling. I should've never told him about the auditions.

Tina spotted me and Ty and stomped over to me, jerking my handlebars so hard that she almost flipped me over like a clumsy circus performer. "Was he at the sign-ups yesterday, Arlie? Because he was waiting for me today. Amber said he'd been there all day."

"Just looking at the little animals, that's all, I swear. You know I'm a pet person."

I sighed. Trey was pathetic and sad, it was true, but enough was enough.

I looked to Ty for help, but he just gave an elaborate shrug and biked off, throwing a grin over his shoulder. He almost collided with a police car that was coming up the street. I got a brain flash.

"Tina, it's okay. I'll explain to Trey, okay?" I gave her a significant look.

Tina rolled her eyes at me. "Whatever." She shook her head and stomped inside. I put my arm around Trey and pulled him to the side.

"Trey, I didn't want to be the one to tell you this, but you need to know. See that police car?"

Trey looked over his shoulder at the car. It had pulled up, down the street from us, and was just idling. "Yeah. So?"

"That's Tina's new boyfriend, okay? She didn't know how to tell you, but I figured it was time you knew. He's really into her, and he's kind of jealous, okay?"

Trey looked at the car nervously. I just hoped when the car door opened it wouldn't be Sheriff Shifflett inside. Or Old Man Jenkins—that would blow everything. He's about eighty, and he pretty much just hangs out at the diner downtown and passes gas. He says he's keeping it safe from the criminal element, but mostly he's just stinking up the place.

"Really? That's her boyfriend?" His face turned bright red and he glared at me. "Is it Shifflett? I knew it!"

Shoot. I should've thought of that. Of course Trey would fixate on Shifflett. "It's not Shifflett, okay? Just get over it. He's . . . he's a deputy. He carries a gun. You don't need that kind of trouble."

Trey seemed to think about it. "Okay. But maybe . . ."

I gave him my best Tina look and it seemed to do the trick.

"Yeah, okay. Who needs her, right? I mean, if she's a cheater and all. Cheating on me with a cop."

Oh, please. Somebody needed a serious beating with a cluestick. "That's right, Trey. She's a cheater. Not nearly good enough for you. Don't waste your time."

Trey nodded and headed off down the street. In the opposite direction from the car, I noticed. I heaved a huge sigh of relief and scurried into the house before he had second thoughts, or before Old Man Jenkins managed to heave his stinky self out of the car.

I ran into the kitchen and shut the door behind me. Tina was sitting at the table with Mr. Boots, who was doing his best impersonation of a centerpiece. "He gone?"

178

"Oh, yeah. I think he's gone for good."

Tina patted Mr. Boots absently. "Thank goodness. I really do not need this right now." She glared at me. "Mr. Boots is having some issues. Say 'I love you,' Mr. Boots."

Mr. Boots could tell it was his cue, that much was obvious. You don't get spontaneous trembling like that without a reason. "Arroo?" he said, looking around.

"Dammit." Tina sighed.

"Well, that was pretty good," I said. "It's closer, anyway."

"Arlie, the auditions are tomorrow. We're dead."

I tried to think of something uplifting and supportive to say that wasn't a flat-out lie, but I couldn't think of anything. I didn't think my pillbug idea would go over well. Thankfully, a knock at the kitchen door pretty much killed the whole Mr. Boots concern.

"Oh, NO WAY!" Tina shrieked, launching herself out of the chair and throwing herself at the door. "GET OUT!" She threw the door open, screaming at the top

179

of her lungs. It would've scared the crap out of Trey, if it had been him. Unfortunately, it wasn't. It was a deputy sheriff.

I blinked. I'd just been making up the whole deputy scenario for Trey, but now I was feeling pretty darn psychic.

Tina made a weird squeak, like she'd swallowed her yell and choked on it. She looked like she felt like a major biscuit. It probably didn't help matters that the deputy was majorly cute. Way cuter than Trey. Heh.

He cleared his throat and looked around awkwardly. "Is this the Jacobs residence?" He pointed at the chewed-up door. "Buck Shifflett sent me. He said you needed some help fixing your door?"

Tina turned bright pink. "Yes, that's right. Sorry about the yelling. I thought—I mean . . ." She was getting pinker by the minute. It wouldn't be long before she reached the I–fell–asleep–in–the–tanning–bed shade of pink, and that would just be embarrassing.

I took pity on her. I mean, my mouth was still working fine. "Sorry about that. Yeah, it's the door. Vandals, you know. And now we've had a problem with the neighbor's cat. Keeps trying to sneak in, and the only way to make him leave is to scream at him. Good thing you got rid of that cat, Tina."

Tina nodded. "That's right. A cat. I don't usually scream. Never."

The deputy smiled. Sheesh, the guy should have been in toothpaste commercials. Tina looked like she was going to pass out.

"Are you new? I didn't know they'd hired a new deputy," I said, trying to keep things conversational while Tina turned back into herself. At this rate, though, I'd need to come up with a one-woman show.

"Yeah, I'm new. Just part time for now. Deputy Jenkins is retiring."

About time, if you ask me. Deputy Hotstuff smiled again, but at Tina. It was like I'd turned into the invisible girl.

"Aren't you a little young to be a deputy? Don't you

have to be, you know, older?" Sure, it was rude. But, come on, if he had a real job, he had to be way too old for Tina, right? And she should know that right off before she got all swoony over some baby-faced old guy.

Deputy Hotstuff actually blushed. "For most places, yeah, you have to be twenty-one. But here you only need to be eighteen." He cleared his throat and smiled at Tina again. "Are you Tina? I'm Ben Reynolds—I think we went to high school together? I graduated two years ago."

Tina smiled this huge sunny smile. She didn't even look like the same person. "Ben! Of course I know you, how are you!" She practically had sunbeams shooting out her pores. "Arlie, this is Ben Reynolds."

Well, yeah, I'm not deaf. But even though Tina's voice was sugary sweet, I can take a hint. "Wow, look at the time. I've got to go upstairs. It's real important." Tina nodded and smiled up at Ben again.

I could've taken off all my clothes and done a conga line with Mr. Boots around the room and I swear they wouldn't have even noticed. I grabbed Mr. Boots and brought him upstairs with me. He really didn't need to see that.

I plopped Mr. Boots down on his bed in the hall for some alone-time and went into my room to do what had become my usual Cuddles check. Thankfully, everything seemed normal and Cuddles-free. I flopped down on the bed to think things over. I had to come up with a new plan, but it had been a pretty stressful week, and it wasn't long before I'd completely conked out.

I woke up suddenly and sat bolt upright. I must've been asleep a long time, because it had gotten dark outside and everything. I had the creepiest feeling, though, like something had just jumped off my bed, and I couldn't figure out what had woken me up.

"Mr. Boots?" I called, but he didn't respond. I listened for a second, and then flopped back onto my pillow. Right onto something weird and hard.

I froze and then slowly reached back to grab whatever I was lying on. When I saw what it was, all I could do was stare. It was Tucker Tannon's head.

183

Okay, not the real Tucker Tannon, but one of those stupid standees from the movie theater. I gave a strangled scream and jumped off the bed, right into a pile of other standee parts—weird decapitated poodles, pieces of Misty Morgan, that little dancing squirrel. It was like a reality-TV nightmare.

I did a spazzy hop over to a clear section of floor and looked back at the bed. That head hadn't been on my pillow when I went to sleep. And there sure as heck hadn't been a big wet patch on the part of the bed that I hadn't been sleeping on. I leaned closer to inspect the patch without getting too close. There were tiny blops of wetness leading off the bed. Almost like footprints.

"Mr. Boots?" I said in a weird strangly voice. I heard a noise in the closet, and turned to look at the half-open door. I didn't blame the guy for not wanting to come out. My room had turned into a freak show. "Mr. Boots?"

I took a step closer and poked at the door to make it open a little wider. I don't know why I was acting so paranoid. I should get a medal for most unreasonable freak-out, right? Mr. Boots was just hiding, it was obvious. In the back corner of the closet, I could see his eyes doing that weird glowy thing that dog eyes do when the light hits them just right.

I didn't like the way he was looking at me, though.

"Mr. Boots? Say 'I love you.'"

"Arroo?"

I heard Mr. Boots's tiny voice, no problem. But it wasn't coming from the closet. It was coming from the hallway. Outside my room.

I turned back to the closet and stared into those weird glowy eyes. I wasn't dreaming. It was real.

I did the only thing I could think of. I made a break for the door, jerked it open as fast as I could, did a running long jump over Mr. Boots in the hallway, and streaked down the stairs.

Sure, Ty's idea was really lousy. Sure, it wouldn't work. But at this point, I didn't care. Things couldn't get much worse. I grabbed the phone and hit speed-dial.

"Ty? It's Arlie. Get a shovel."

CHAPTER 11

"I'M STILL NOT SURE ABOUT THIS, TY," I SAID, spitting out a leaf from the shrubs near Mandy's house. We'd been crouching there for what seemed like an hour, just waiting to make sure everybody had gone to bed, and I was a little more up close and personal with the shrubbery than I like. All I can say is, thank God for adrenaline.

"Hey, you called me, remember? I was like, fine, you don't want to do it, we don't do it." Ty poked me in the ribs with the end of his shovel.

"Maybe I'm reconsidering."

Ty shook his head. "Oh no, you don't. I snuck out in the middle of the night, Arlie. I took my dad's special shovel. You know what he'll do if he finds out? You're crazy if you think you're backing out now."

I sighed. I'd snuck out too, but I knew it didn't really count. I'd just waited until Tina had gone to her room. It's not like anyone would really catch me.

"Arrr-arr-oo," Mr. Boots grumbled.

"I love you too, Mr. Boots," I said. "Now, quiet."

Ty shot me and Mr. Boots a dirty look. I hadn't been big on bringing the chatty Chihuahua along either, but it's not like I had much choice. Ever since it had clicked with him that Tina liked him to talk, he'd been getting mouthier and mouthier. He'd totally busted me while I was making my discreet exit, and he wouldn't shut up about it. He would've broadcast the news to the whole neighborhood if I hadn't shoved him in my backpack.

I shifted my weight and grabbed the shovel from Ty. "Let's do this, then."

Crouching down, we made our way over to the line of graves out by Mandy's house. Funny, I'd never realized how menacing happy dancing frogs could be. These really managed to pull it off, too. With all the froufrou decorations, Mandy's house totally looked like something out of a fairy tale. And it suddenly hit me—don't a lot of fairy tales end with someone getting eaten? Maybe this was a bad idea.

We'd brought a flashlight to read the names, but now shining it willy-nilly around the yard seemed like a bad plan. I'd been worried about getting caught and hauled in by the cops, but these creepy frogs were making me think that cops were the least of our problems. We were dealing with the undead, after all.

"Do you remember which one was Poppy?" If we were going to do this, I had to stop thinking about the whole undead thing. I thought Poppy was one of the smiling bumblebees, but I wasn't sure.

"Butterfly, right? Here it is." Ty pointed at one of the graves and immediately stabbed his shovel into the ground. Looked like somebody was as eager to get this over with as I was.

I ducked a shovelful of flying grass and peered at the name stenciled on the butterfly's tummy. Something wasn't quite right. I looked closer and then dove for Ty's shovel, almost dislocating my arm in the process.

"Ty, stop it, you dork—that's not Poppy!" Great. Not only were we grave robbers, but we were incompetent grave robbers. The last thing we needed was to dig up one of Cuddles's enemies.

Ty leaned in to look at the butterfly. "Sure, see? P-O-L . . . oh, shoot. Polly. That's not good."

"No kidding." I started shoving the dirt back into the hole and tried to pat the ground back down, but I don't think it looked the way it had before. I just hoped Polly wasn't a vindictive little whatever she was.

We were definitely going to have to risk the flash-light. I stuck it under my shirt and turned it on, hoping that way, we'd get enough light to read the markers by, but not enough to alert the neighbors. Luckily, enough of the light shone through my T-shirt so we could read the names. Apparently it also shone up under my face and really freaked Ty out, because he jumped about ten feet in the air. Mr. Boots came this close to being roadkill.

I smirked and tapped at the happy bumblebee at the end. "Poppy."

"Holy cow, Arlie, turn that thing off. You trying to give me a heart attack?" Ty had never been good at camp when the scary stories started.

"Wow, kinda jumpy there, aren't you, Ty? Nervous?" I made a face that I hoped would be especially ghoulish, and then snapped the flashlight off.

Ty scowled at me and stabbed his shovel into the ground. "Let's just dig this sucker up."

We got to work digging, and I have to say, it didn't go the way I'd thought. Novice digger that I am, I'd been thinking we'd be there half an hour, tops. But after that top layer of grass came up, we were just getting tiny little dusty shovelfuls. Which would have been okay if Mandy had been a shallow-grave kind of girl. I'm thinking one, two inches tops would've been nice. Naturally she wasn't. I'd gotten blisters on both hands before I threw my shovel down and collapsed onto the lawn. I don't even know whose grave I was sitting on.

"Hey, what gives?" Ty said, still shoveling.

"This is hopeless. We're never going to get to Poppy. Who knows if she's even in there? Mandy could've been lying to us."

I sighed heavily. Mr. Boots came over and licked my cheek. I think he was just in it for the salt, though—I was sweating like a pig.

Ty shook his head and kept on going. "We're doing well, Arlie. We're really close, okay? I think I felt something hard down there."

I rolled my eyes at him. "So what else is new? The whole ground is hard. We need to come up with a new plan."

"No, I'm serious, Arlie—listen." He tapped his shovel around a couple of times and then I heard it. I'm not sure what it was, but it was definitely a not-dirt sound.

I heaved myself back up and picked up the shovel. Call me what you want, but I'm not a quitter. At least not when I can see the finish line. I started scraping dirt away from the middle, but I had nothing on Ty—he was like some out-of-control digging machine.

Ty wiped his forehead. "Can you see it? I think it's a can."

I peered into the hole. There was definitely a can-shaped lump in the middle. It had to be Poppy.

"See? Right there." Ty knocked at the lump with the edge of his shovel and I heard it give a hollow *clang*. Unfortunately, I wasn't the only one who heard it, because at that moment a light came on in the house.

"Crap, Ty, someone's awake!" I ducked down, as if that would make a difference. If we were busted, we were busted. Ducking behind a smiling sunflower wasn't going to help.

Ty shook his head. "No problem—I've almost got it." He reached down into the hole and tried to pry the can out, but it wasn't working—it was still too buried. I grabbed Ty by the shirt and dragged him down just as a light came on downstairs.

"Are you crazy? There's somebody up!" I hissed. I did not want to get caught out here. There's no way Sheriff Shifflett would be able to overlook a grave-robbing expedition.

"Arlie, we can just grab it and run! We've got enough time." Ty tried to get his shirt free, but I had it in a death grip. "Cut it out!"

"We can't just run—she'll see the holes and know it's us!" If we were going to get caught, I'd rather get it over with. That way, we at least had a shot of talking our way out of it.

The light came on, on the back porch. We huddled down next to the grave markers and hoped that whoever it was wouldn't come outside. There wasn't much cover around there, and the only one who could even think about hiding in that hole was Mr. Boots. And he was too busy chewing on his hind foot to be thinking about escape routes.

The back door opened, and Mandy stepped out on the porch, carrying Puffkins in her arms. She stopped and looked around for a minute, and then dumped him onto the front stoop.

"See? Nobody out here, you silly cat. Now have a fun night and I'll see you in the morning." Mandy patted the lump that was Puffkins on the head and went back inside.

Puffkins didn't move a muscle as the light snapped off on the back porch. I sat up and watched. The light in the kitchen went off—still no Puffkins movement. When the light went off upstairs, I got up and brushed the dirt off my pants.

"So do you think that cat just lies there all night? Weird." I brushed stray dirt off my shirt.

"Probably," Ty said, going back to the hole to try to work the can free.

I watched him for a couple of seconds, and then looked over at Puffkins. "Ty, holy crap," I breathed.

Puffkins had stood up and was sniffing the wind. Then he turned his head and looked right at me.

For some reason, it really creeped me out. Grave robbing is one thing, but having a witness is something completely different. "He totally knows we're here. And he's moving and everything. He's seen us digging."

"Wow," Ty said, but he wasn't even paying attention. It looked like he's gotten one end of the can loose. I turned back to Puffkins. That cat better not blow our cover.

Puffkins started toward us, never taking his eyes off me. He was doing that stalking walk, just like any regular cat would. Like he did it all the time. It was the weirdest thing ever.

When Puffkins was about ten feet away, Mr. Boots stopped chewing his foot and noticed him. And dorky dog that he is, he just strolled up to say hello. As if Puffkins wanted to play.

Puffkins stopped dead still and stared at Mr. Boots for a second, like he was considering ripping his head off and chucking it around like a soccer ball. Then he suddenly went completely limp and flopped down on the ground in his best stuffed-animal impression. Mr. Boots started in shock and then looked around all embarrassed, like it wasn't his fault.

"So it's all an act," I said to Ty. "Puffkins is as active as any other cat when he wants to be."

Mr. Boots sat down and nosed Puffkins nervously. He didn't even seem to be breathing. This was ridiculous.

"Okay, Puffkins, you can cut the act. We know you move, okay?" I wasn't going to sit there and watch Mr. Boots sweat like he was waiting for the "you break it, you bought it" rule to take effect.

After a couple of seconds, Puffkins raised his head and glared at me, and then hauled himself up. Mr. Boots apparently had had enough, because he hightailed it over to the other side of the grave.

"How's it going?" I asked, peering into the hole.

"Got it." Ty held up the can triumphantly. It looked just like the one Cuddles had been buried in—one of those fancy tea cans.

"And the bones are inside?" I asked.

Ty shook the can lightly and it made a rattling noise that really made me want to lose my lunch. Then he handed the can to me.

"You do the honors. You couldn't pay me enough to open that thing."

I gave him a dirty look and pulled at the top of the can. It wasn't like with Cuddles—it popped right open. I turned my flashlight on and peeked inside.

"So?" Ty looked nervous. "Any note? Are we cursed again?"

I shook my head as I put the lid back on. "Just bones, it looks like. We can take a closer look when we're out of here. But we'd better hurry."

Me and Ty started shoveling dirt back into the hole as fast as we could, and it wasn't long before we'd gotten it all filled up. But boy, was it obvious that Poppy's grave had been defiled.

"She's totally going to know," I said, staring at the big ugly mound of dirt. You didn't even need a flashlight to know it was bad.

197

"We're so busted," Ty said, looking around for some way to disguise it. "Maybe one of those garden gnomes?"

"Ty, a garden gnome is not going to hide the big pile o' dirt. It'll just look more suspicious."

Ty nodded. "Don't suppose you've got any sod on you?" He grinned at me like he was trying to joke about it, but it wasn't really funny.

"Does Mandy know our names? I can't remember if we ever told her," I said, grasping at straws. Like she couldn't figure it out in about two seconds.

Ty snapped his fingers. "I've got it." He skipped over to where Puffkins was watching us and he scooped him up. Puffkins was so shocked, he didn't even go limp, he just stared at Ty and patted his arm with his paws. It may have been a wimpy cat version of a smackdown—I'm not sure.

Ty carried Puffkins over to the graves, plopped him smack down in the middle of the dirt, and started rubbing it all over his feet. Puffkins stared at him in horror, and I have to admit, I probably had the same expression.

"Ty, you're getting him filthy!" I said. Puffkins was nothing but white fluffy hair, and now his entire lower legs were a gross dark matted color.

"That's the idea! Mandy'll think Puffkins did this." Ty chuckled to himself and held Puffkins up for display. "Look dirty enough?"

Puffkins had been admirably restrained through all this, but now he turned his head deliberately and glared at Ty for a long second. Then he licked his lips, opened his mouth, and shrieked.

It was a huge bloodcurdling shriek—way too big for a cat like that. If you'd told me Puffkins was part mountain lion and part opera singer, I would've believed you in a heartbeat.

Ty dropped Puffkins like a hot potato and started grabbing his stuff. "Out of here! Now! Run!"

I shoved Mr. Boots into my backpack, tucked Poppy's can under my arm, and we took off running just as lights started snapping on all over that house.

We didn't stop until I thought my heart was going

to explode in my chest and Mr. Boots was going to hurl puppy chow all over the back of my shirt. We definitely should have brought our bikes.

"Aren't you glad we didn't bring bikes?" Ty said, slinging the shovel over his shoulder jauntily. "They would've seen us for sure."

I would've had a good comeback for that if my lungs hadn't been trying to crawl up my throat and out onto the pavement to get more air.

"Let's head over to Main Street—we can use the streetlamps to get a look at Poppy there."

I nodded. Not that I thought it was actually a good idea—seemed to me that walking on Main Street in the middle of the night would be just asking for trouble. But arguing would take breath, and I didn't have any to spare at the moment. Ty made a big display of waiting patiently while I stopped wheezing and then we headed downtown.

We were a couple of blocks away when I noticed how weird things looked. I'd never realized streetlamps were so darn bright. Seems like they could save a little energy and take them down a couple of hundred notches, but that's just me.

"Man, how much light do they need down here?" I said to Ty. He was definitely going to attract attention, what with the dirt and shovel and all. And let's not even mention the fact that I was carrying a dead body.

Ty stopped short and looked worried. "Something's not right, Arlie. Do you smell that? That burny smell?"

I sniffed. It did smell strange, actually. A heavy smoky smell. "Something's on fire?"

Ty nodded and we kept going, keeping to the shadowy parts of the street. Not that there were many. We'd only gone about half a block more when we saw it.

"Oh, man, talk about a fire . . ." One of the stores on Main Street was lit up like a torch. We ducked around a corner to get a closer view.

It was Knoble's Olde-Tyme Ice Cream Shoppe. Flames were shooting out of the ceiling, and the front window was completely gone. But the thing that really caught my attention was the front door. It hadn't caught fire yet, but it was already destroyed. Huge chunks were missing. Like something had taken repeated whacks at it.

I could feel the heat of the flames from our hiding spot, but I felt like I'd gotten a face full of ice water. I turned to Ty, and he looked as freaked out as I felt. "The door, Ty. Look at the door."

Ty's eyes were huge. "I saw. The window, too. But you didn't go to the ice cream shop. Did you?"

I shook my head. "You said I shouldn't get ice cream. Because of Cuddles."

"So why would Cuddles go there?"

I shrugged and hugged Poppy's can closer to my chest. Mr. Boots took one look at the fire and crawled deeper into my backpack. Smart dog.

"We'd better get out of here." Ty picked his shovel back up and started back down the alley.

I followed, babbling like an idiot. "But it doesn't make sense! That was Cuddles, right? He did that? But why the fire? And I didn't go for ice cream! Did he go there just because I mentioned it?"

Ty stopped and gave me a hard look. "Quiet, Arlie. We'll figure it out, but not right now. Now we have to get home. If anyone sees us, we're finished."

Ty was right. The last thing I needed was for Sheriff Shifflett to catch me right now. Because that's all the evidence he'd need to put me away for good.

CHAPTER 12

I DIDN'T WASTE ANY TIME WHEN I GOT HOME.
I shot up the stairs two at a time and chucked
Poppy's can into the middle of my bed. Then I
cleaned myself up and headed back downstairs
for an oh so restful night on the couch. If Cuddles
wanted my closet, fine. He could have the
whole stinkin' room.

If Tina wondered why I was conked out on
the sofa the next morning, she didn't say anything about it. I woke up to the sounds of her
coaching Mr. Boots in the kitchen. Apparently
it wasn't going well. Unless the sounds "squik"

and "rawrrr" are parts of the phrase "I love you" that I'm not aware of. Which, at this point, I was totally willing to believe.

I had pretty much decided to spend the day sinking slowly into the cushions with the loose change when someone knocked on the door. Not that that got me up, actually, but Tina coming in with Ty made me act a little more alert.

"She's right there. See if you can do anything with her, okay? I don't want to have to dig under the sofa cushions to find her when our parents get back." Tina rolled her eyes at me and headed back into the kitchen.

Sure, I'd been vegetating on the couch for most of the morning, but I felt that was uncalled for. I was planning to move eventually. I was just waiting until the happy reunion had taken place in my room and my undead friends had gone far, far away. I was more than willing to wait them out.

Ty sat down on the cushion near my feet. "I brought the papers, Arlie. It's not good."

I shook my head. "I don't even want to see them, okay?"

Ty snorted. "Well, tough luck. I had to read them, you do too. First the reputable press."

He threw the paper at me and I picked it up, mostly because the corner was poking into my nose in a painful way. I looked at the headline.

VANDALS STRIKE AGAIN! FOURTH KNOBLE ESTABLISHMENT TARGETED

I threw the paper back at Ty. "Tell me something I don't know."

Ty picked it up. "It says here that the vandals trashed the ice cream shop and totally destroyed everything, but mostly targeted papers in the back office. Then they torched the place. Weird, huh?"

I closed my eyes. "Yeah. Weird. I'll remind Cuddles not to play with matches."

Ty nudged me on the leg. "It's just . . . it doesn't sound

like Cuddles so much. Not really his style, you know? Maybe we're wrong?"

I sat up and smacked Ty in the stomach with my pillow, which I instantly regretted, mostly because he didn't give it back. "It was him, okay? You need evidence? Fine. Just wait a couple of hours and I'm sure my room will be filled to the brim with melty ice cream and scoopers galore." I flopped back down on the sofa and closed my eyes again.

"Okay, then take a look at this one." He waved a newspaper an inch from my face until I opened my eyes again. I snatched it away. It was the *Daily Squealer.*

GLOWING CREATURE STILL UNIDENTIFIED; PET PSYCHIC CALLED IN.

"So what. A pet psychic. Great."

Ty sighed. "Read the first line, okay?"

I looked again and read aloud. "'The glowing creature responsible for the destruction of three Knoble businesses continues to elude experts and, strangely, was not seen during last night's vandalism of Knoble's Olde-Tyme Ice Cream Shoppe.'"

I dropped the paper onto the floor. "So?"

"So they didn't see Cuddles there last night. Maybe he wasn't there?"

I sat up again and snatched my pillow back from Ty. "They just didn't see him, Ty. That doesn't mean he wasn't there. It's hard to see glowy eyes in the middle of a fire."

"I don't know, Arlie . . ." Ty picked up the paper and folded it neatly. He shook his head. "This last one—it doesn't seem right to me."

"This whole thing doesn't seem right to me, Ty! I'm sleeping on the stinkin' couch, waking up every five seconds afraid that some undead hamster who loves me will show up. Is that right? I don't think so."

Ty nodded. "Point taken. Any news about Poppy? Any . . . uh . . . activity there?"

I sighed. "I don't know. She's in my room. Let's go check."

I stood up and almost tripped on Mr. Boots, who had come skittering into the room in a panic. Tina was close on his heels.

"Not going well?" I said.

"I don't know what's wrong with him. He's not concentrating. He can't say anything! It's like he's half asleep."

Me and Ty exchanged guilty glances. It probably hadn't been the best idea to keep Mr. Boots up the night before his big break. But there was nothing we could do about it now.

Tina sank down onto the couch. "Seriously, is it so hard? What is so difficult about saying 'I love you'?"

"Arr-oo-ee," said Mr. Boots mournfully.

"That's great, Mr. Boots, but not even close." Tina sighed. Mr. Boots grumbled something that was definitely not "I love you" under his breath and took off for the stairs. "Let him go, it doesn't even matter."

"Sure, it does. Maybe there's something else he can do."

Tina snorted. "Yeah, right. The only thing that comes naturally to that dog is nude modeling."

I patted Tina awkwardly on the arm. "We'll get him and then we'll think of something."

Ty and I headed upstairs. "Poor Tina," I whispered. "Mr. Boots is going to suck."

"Well, Ted'll be so much better than everyone else, maybe it won't matter." Ty hesitated at the top of the stairs. "So they're together? In your room?"

"I guess so. She's in there, at least." The door was partway open and I pushed it with my foot. There, on my bed, was the can. The lid was off, and a small shape was sitting right next to it.

"MR. BOOTS! NO!" I screeched and dove for the bed. Mr. Boots had worked the lid off Poppy's can and was nose-deep inside.

He pricked his ears up and looked at me, but he didn't stop with the sniffing. A leg bone was sticking out of the can. At least I think it was a leg bone. What-ever it was, it was still skeletal and extremely disturbing.

Seriously, that image is never going to leave my head.

Ty gave a flying leap and grabbed Mr. Boots by the legs, dragging him away from the can. I grabbed the Tucker Tannon standee head and used it to shove the tiny bones back into the can. Then I did a huge repulsed gross-out dance.

"They're still bones, Ty! Still bones!" I then continued on to freak-out dance, part two.

"Drop it, Mr. Boots! Drop it! Give!" Ty shook Mr. Boots upside down until Mr. Boots horked up one last little bone.

Whatever it was, I scooped it back into the can with the Tucker Tannon head. I didn't really look at it. Just get it back in the can, that's all I cared about. Ty had crouched down and was doing deep breaths, like not passing out was all he cared about.

Once we were sure Mr. Boots had given up the goods, and all the bones were back in the can with the lid on tight, I looked around. Sure, the place was a mess, filled with standee parts and some stray pieces of popcorn. But as far as I could tell, there was no ice cream paraphernalia anywhere.

Ty put Mr. Boots down onto the floor and looked around. "This the closet?"

I nodded.

Ty peeked inside. "He's not in here now. Maybe he and Poppy had a fight?"

"I don't know," I said, sinking down onto the bed. "No gifts, though. Maybe he's over me?"

"Or maybe it wasn't him." Ty sat down too. Good thing Mrs. Knoble wasn't here—she would've freaked out. "Don't worry. We'll figure it out."

"I've got it!" Tina's voice boomed up the stairs. "Mr. Boots! I've got it!"

Tina came barreling into the room carrying a tiny top hat and a fistful of Mr. Boots's old clothes.

"What is he good at? Being naked, right? So what is his talent?" She looked at me significantly. "Striptease. He's going to be a doggie stripper. Gypsy Rose Boots. I'll get the clothes on him, put the doggie stripper-pole

212

up, and play the song 'You Can Leave Your Hat On.' Or maybe that stripper song, what's it called?"

"'The Stripper'?" Ty said, glancing at me nervously.

"Right! Then he gets down to taking it all off. What do you think? Good? It's perfect right?"

I had to admit, it made sense. I'd seen Mr. Boots taking clothes off, and he really was talented at that. So the idea of him stripping with a pole was a little disturbing. So what? As long as it worked for Tina and didn't get us arrested, I was all for it.

"That's much better than saying 'I love you,'" I said, nodding.

"Arr–ooff-oo?" Mr. Boots said thoughtfully.

"No, forget that, Mr. Boots," Tina said, looking down at him. "It's all about the attitude now." She frowned at a piece of standee on the floor. "Is that Tucker Tannon's head?"

"Don't ask." There were some things I'd never be able to explain.

"Okay, never mind. Come on, Mr. Boots! We've got

work to do!" She grabbed Mr. Boots under the arms and pranced out of the room.

I headed out after her. Somehow, hanging out in my room had lost all appeal for me since it had become a haven for the supernatural forces of evil.

I went down to the kitchen table and helped myself to one of Suzette's cookies. Mrs. Knoble had gone all out since we saw her last, and was constantly leaving offerings of food on the back step like some kind of benevolent meal fairy. I wasn't complaining, though.

"So what's the situation, Ty? What have we got here?"

I held the cookie tin out to Ty.

"Beats me. This Poppy thing may still work—just give it a chance."

I gaped at him. "Ty, she's been there for hours! And she's still just a pile of bones. Heck, I wouldn't go out with her, why should we expect Cuddles to?"

Ty rolled his eyes. "He's a hamster, Arlie. They have different standards, okay?"

I threw down my cookie in disgust. There are some things that even frosted chocolate chocolate chip won't fix. "Great. So in the meantime I just get used to being a magnet for mayhem and get to know my new roommate?"

"I don't see that you have any choice, okay?" Ty picked up my discarded cookie and scarfed it down. I pretended to barf. Seriously, what a pig.

"Mr. Boots! Come back!" Tina screamed from upstairs.

Ty raised his eyebrows. "Trouble in paradise?"

"Get out of there. Mr. Boots? What are you— eeeewww!" Tina's shriek got both me and Ty up out of our chairs, because we had a pretty good idea what that last "eeww" meant. Somebody wouldn't leave the secret bone stash alone.

We got to the stairs just as Mr. Boots came clattering down. He was wearing a tasteful Chinese-style blouse, but I wasn't really concerned about his fashion sense right then. Because in his mouth, he was carrying the can full of Poppy's bones.

He must've somehow gotten the lid off again, because he was holding it by the rim, nose right in there with good ol' Poppy. He threw a dismissive glance at me and then disappeared around the corner.

Tina came lumbering down after him. "What the heck was that? Was that bones? Arlie, you are so weird. Are you going goth or something?"

I opened my mouth to say something, but Tina wasn't even paying attention.

"Where did he go? We don't have time for this—the auditions are in a few hours!"

I pointed around the corner. "Look, I can explain, I just need that can back, okay?" I could give a crap about the auditions—the can was the only important thing at this point. Cuddles may not have warmed up to Poppy right away, but I had a feeling he'd be pretty darn pissed if Mr. Boots scarfed her down for lunch.

Tina didn't even answer. She just disappeared around the corner. She stormed back a few seconds later.

"Okay, did he come back through here?"

I shook my head. This was definitely not good. Mr. Boots has a million hiding places in this house, and even though we know about most of them, he knows how to disappear if he needs to.

We separated and covered the house, but no matter what we did, we couldn't find Mr. Boots. I retrieved the can lid, but it was pretty much no good without the actual can. Eventually me and Ty retreated to the kitchen, where we decided our best bet was to sit on the floor under the table and eat cookies. That way we'd attract the least amount of Tina attention, and it had the advantage of being a location where we could legitimately claim to be on the lookout for Mr. Boots. Ty said we were undercover, and I didn't disagree. I had a terrible feeling that whatever Mr. Boots was going to do with those bones was already done at this point.

Of course it was too much to hope that Tina wouldn't catch on. We still had three cookies left when Tina dragged a chair out from under the table, grabbed me by the collar, and hauled me out.

"Where is he, Arlie?" she said, pulling me to my feet.

"I really don't know. We were watching for him. In case he went by."

"It's a stakeout." Ty's voice floated up from under the table.

"Well, your stakeout is officially over. I have one hour before the auditions start. Now I need to find Mr. Boots, get him into his outfit, and get him there. And you're going to help, okay?"

I nodded. Couldn't see any problem with that. Other than the fact that I had no idea where the sucker could be, that is.

"Have you tried asking him to say 'I love you'? Maybe he'll forget he's hiding and say it back."

Tina shook her head. "Already tried that. But don't worry. Finding Mr. Boots is my problem. All you've got to do is go down to the auditorium and stall them."

"What?" Finding Mr. Boots was one thing. Going down and exposing a television viewing audience to a cranky Cuddles, that was something else.

"You heard me. Go down there. Sign him in. Tell them he's arriving late, you know, finding his center and all. They'll buy it. We'll be there by his call time, I promise."

I shook my head no. "I can't go. I can't do it. Sorry, Tina, I'll find him, if you want. But I can't go down there."

"Bad things will happen." Ty's voice floated up again. He seriously needed to get out from under that table.

"Ty's right. Bad things will happen. I need to stay here." There was no way I was going down to that auditorium.

Tina's eyes narrowed. "Bad things will happen if you stay here, trust me on that, Arlie. Your choice, though."

I looked at Tina. She would make my life miserable if I stayed there. And it's not like I had any clue where to find Mr. Boots. At least with Cuddles I had a fighting chance, right?

I brushed the dust off my butt and pulled out the chair near Ty. "Come on, Ty, we're going to the auditorium. We need to stall."

Ty shot out from under the table at warp speed. I couldn't help but notice that he'd finished off the last of the cookies. Of course. "Are you crazy, Arlie? You can't go down there! Think about it!"

Tina crossed her arms and glared at me.

"I've thought about it, Ty. We're going. Come on."

Tina gave me a huge hug that shocked me so much, I almost wet myself. "Just stall them, Arlie, and we'll be there. I promise."

I nodded. "Okay. We'll stall them."

I grabbed Ty by the arm and dragged him out of the house. This was it. I didn't know what Cuddles was going to do, but I was about to find out.

CHAPTER *13*

I TRIED TO LOOK ON THE BRIGHT SIDE. SURE, I was bringing a hostile and verifiably violent hamster with superpowers to my school auditorium, where he would come face-to-face with his former owner, untalented animals, and some very scary television personalities. Best-case scenario? He tears the place apart in the wee hours and the first day of school is pushed back a few months. Worst-case scenario? I didn't want to think about it.

Me and Ty braced ourselves, exchanged significant looks, and did a quick fist-bump before going inside. Why we did the fist-bump, I have no idea. We'd never done one before. I think it made us feel tougher somehow.

Inside was pure mayhem. They'd managed to pull together about a million more Tucker Tannon and Misty Morgan standees, and the whole entryway was decked out. Everywhere I looked, nervous, pasty-looking people were clutching stressed-out shedding pets. The room was filled with the sounds of cats with hairballs and dogs with nervous conditions.

I pushed through what seemed like a wall of fur and tried to find the check-in table. Amber and Beulah had set up in a corner, and they were smiling so hard, their faces looked like they might rip in two. Actually, check that. Amber was smiling. Beulah was smoking like a chimney and scowling.

I hurried over to the table. "Hey, Amber, just checking in." I tried to look cheery and like someone who had a pet.

Amber turned her megawatt smile to me, but her eyes

looked panicked. "Hey, Arlie! Hi! Where are Tina and Mr. Boots?" Amber had that look that substitute teachers tend to get after lunch, when they figure out there's still half a day left to go. Maybe this wasn't a dream job after all.

"You look great, Amber! Great hair. Do I register with you?" I figured the best course of action would be to pile on the flattery and totally ignore Amber's questions. Maybe then she wouldn't notice that Mr. Boots was nowhere to be seen.

"Yeah, but it really should be Tina. Is she here?" Amber's smiled faded a little bit.

Beulah snorted and leaned back in her chair, blowing smoke at the ceiling. "Troublemaker."

"I'll just sign in for Tina, if you don't mind. Mr. Boots is finding his center." I grabbed the pen out of Amber's hand. "Where do I sign?"

Amber looked around behind me. "Are they here? I don't see them." She pursed her lips at me. I was turning into a problem. And Amber doesn't like problems.

"Oh, they're over there," I said, and waved my hand at the crowd. "See? Sign right here?" I took the clipboard out of her hand.

Amber frowned. "But, Arlie—"

Ty pushed past me and leaned into Amber's face. "Look, Amber, this is a big deal for Mr. Boots, okay? He's had offers from the networks. He's got a lot of pressure on him. He's taking a moment to free his inner Boots. He's finding his center. He's going to his happy place."

Amber looked doubtful. "Freeing his inner Boots?"

Beulah started making this raspy laugh, but ended up choking instead. Smoke came out of her nose and everything.

"I'll just sign in and go help him with his warm-up exercises, 'kay?" I chirped, putting a big checkmark next to Mr. Boots's name. I handed the clipboard back to Amber.

Amber nodded doubtfully. After all, I'd checked the sheet. Not much she could do now. "Okay, well, it's not long before we get started. This area is the green room area, where the animals all wait. And the cameras are set up in the auditorium for the auditions. Mr. Boots is right after Puffkins, so get ready to set up when Mandy goes onstage, okay?"

I nodded and quickly disappeared back into the crowd. I looked around nervously. Little tufts of hair were sticking to my shoes. Somebody'd had an accident on the floor. This was definitely not anyone's happy place. At least it didn't seem like Cuddles was particularly upset to be here. He wasn't trashing the place, anyway, so that was something. I was starting not to care what he did after we left.

"Man, she'd better get here," Ty breathed. We stationed ourselves near the door so we could keep an eye out for Tina. What I didn't realize was that we'd also stationed ourselves next to Mandy.

"Hey, guys! I thought I'd see you here. Where's your dog?" Mandy looked around like she expected him to pop out of my pocket or from behind Ty's sneaker.

225

"He's not here yet. Just getting ready. You know, mental preparations and all. How's Puffkins handling this?"

Mandy motioned to Puffkins, who was slumped against the window. He was wearing a stars-and-stripes vest and cape.

"Very patriotic," Ty said, eyeing Puffkins nervously. He didn't need to worry, though. Puffkins didn't bat an eye, let alone start pointing a shaking, accusatory paw in Ty's direction.

"Oh my God, he is freaking out," Mandy gushed. "He is totally out of control, I just hope he calms down before the auditions."

I looked down at Puffkins again. Yup, no movement. Nothing. If that's freaking out, I'd hate to see placid. "Really? He looks like he's handling it okay."

Mandy shook her head. "He had a total panic attack last night. You wouldn't believe. He wanted to go out, right? So I let him out and then next thing you know, he's gone crazy, screaming and trying to dig up all my old pets. It was pretty freaky. He's never done anything like that before. He had to have a whole makeover this morning."

"Man, that's really weird," I said, not able to meet Mandy's eyes. Poor cat. I can't believe Mandy bought our lame scenario.

"Yeah, no kidding. He's doing an all-American routine, though, so hopefully his high spirits and extra energy won't hurt him too much."

I nodded again. Not much you can say when you hear those words applied to a living, breathing throw rug. Mandy shot me a suspicious look and gathered up a small duffel bag filled with props. "What's your dog doing? You're not doing all-American too, are you? Puffkins is flame-retardant! His whole costume, totally one hundred percent not flammable."

I shook my head. "Nope, definitely not all-American. Or flame-retardant."

Ty snickered, but I shot him a look. I was starting to think that a doggie striptease might be a really bad idea.

"Is your dog coming soon?" Mandy asked, looking at the clock. "I think they're starting any minute."

"Just like Tina to make a dramatic entrance, huh, Arlie?" I heard a smug voice behind me. I shook my head and turned around.

"Trey. Why am I not surprised?" I really wasn't, that was the pathetic thing. "This is a pet audition, remember? You probably shouldn't be here."

Trey smirked. "My pet's auditioning. See my pet? This is Sparky." He held up his iguana friend from the other day. Sparky swiveled his eye around and shot me a look that said he'd never in his life gone by any name as undignified as "Sparky." I felt kind of bad for the guy.

"Sparky, that's great. What's his talent?" I shifted nervously. Tina was going to freak when she got here and saw Trey. As if she wouldn't already be freaking enough.

"I figured he'd eat some bugs. He's real good at that." Sparky gave an iguana eye roll and slapped Trey in the face.

228

"He's really cute!" Mandy said, patting Sparky on the head. "I'm Mandy, and this is Puffkins." She scooped up Puffkins and waggled him in front of Sparky. I think they exchanged a look of shared misery, but maybe I'm just projecting.

"Wow. Mandy. Hi. I'm, uh, Trey? You new around here?" Trey flipped the hair out of his eyes in a supercool move that seriously ticked off Sparky, who immediately started clawing at the air in a slow-motion attempt to escape.

Mandy giggled and looked up at Trey through her eyelashes. Oh man, not this again. I rolled my eyes at Ty, who stifled a grin. "Well, you two kids should get to know each other. I've got a thing. At the place. With a guy."

Ty nodded. "What she said." We scurried over to the other side of the door to escape the gag-inducing sight of Trey trying to flirt. I couldn't help but smile, though—the prospect of Trey with a parrot on his shoulder and a pair of sparkly deelyboppers on his head made it all worthwhile. I made a mental note to spend some quality time lurking around Mandy's house with a digital camera and a wireless connection to the Internet.

I'd just gotten settled at the door when Amber went to the front of the room and clapped her hands. "Okay, everybody, it's time to get started!" I pressed my face against the window so I could see more of the street, but no Tina. I suddenly had a cold feeling in the pit of my stomach. I didn't have any clue how I was supposed to stall them if Tina didn't show. It's not like I could just ask Cuddles to do something. And I don't think trashing the place would count as a talent, anyway.

"To judge our auditions, I am so honored to introduce Misty Morgan and Tucker Tannon!" Amber squealed, clapping so hard, I thought she'd break her hands. There was a collective gasp as Misty and Tucker came into the room.

I like to think I'm immune to the whole Hollywood thing, but it was really hard not to stare. It was so weird seeing them in real life, you know? Plus, they were both a lot shorter than I expected. And they looked even fakier in real life. I'm guessing it was because of the cameras in the other room, but Misty had makeup five inches deep. Actually, come to think of it, Tucker did too. It was either the cameras or some serious skin condition, and I decided to be charitable.

"Thanks, you guys, for coming out today! I know you're all excited, so I want to wish you the best of luck. Now a couple of ground rules, okay?" Misty cocked her head and looked at us like a beagle begging to go out.

"OKAY!" Amber shrieked, jumping up and down a little. I was kind of embarrassed for her.

"First off, we can't get involved with the contestants, no matter how much we want to, so no touching. Got it?"

Amber nodded and started a round of applause.

"And that also means we can't pet little Rex or Fluffy, got it?" Misty said it like she was doing a cheer.

Amber cheered too, and gave a couple of little hops,

like one of those frog toys attached to a squeezy bulb.

"Misty hates pets," Ty said out of the side of his mouth. I nodded.

"That means no contact at all, unfortunately, so no licking, nothing like that. If we get licked, your little friend is out, got it? It's all about the no-fraternization rule." Tucker gave a big smile and nodded to us all.

"Definite dog hater. Probably had a bowl full of puppies for lunch," Ty whispered. I tried to keep a straight face. The last thing I wanted to do was attract attention and incur the wrath of the mighty forces of the Network Peroxide Gang.

"This is all about having fun, okay? But remember: We're all here to work, so no autographs, no pictures—okay? Good! Now let's get going here! Yay!" Misty and Tucker started cheering and clapping and generally doing what I like to think of as a perfect Kermit the Frog impression. I have to say, they didn't bowl me over.

"Still no Tina," Ty said, checking the window. "What are you going to do?"

I shrugged. This was turning into the worst week ever.

Tucker and Misty disappeared into the auditorium and everyone else gathered in nervous clusters.

Amber went back to the front with her clipboard. "Okay, first off is Marty Bollinger? With Patrick the talking parrot?"

I craned my neck to look. I knew Marty from school, but I hadn't seen him there. Heck, I didn't even know he had a parrot.

Marty hustled to the front of the room with Patrick.

"Thanks, Amber! Ready, Patrick?" Marty beamed at Patrick, who looked like he was suffering from a chronic bout of mange.

Patrick took one look at Amber and let loose with a string of the dirtiest cusswords I've ever heard in my life. Seriously, I don't even know what half of them meant.

Amber turned hot pink and gaped at Marty. "What did he say to me?"

Patrick thoughtfully repeated himself.

Amber's mouth dropped open. "Is that what he's going to say? Is that his talent?"

Marty glanced nervously at Patrick. "Well, sort of. I mean, some of that was new. I don't know where he picked that up."

Amber hugged her clipboard and shook her head at Marty. "I can't put him on to say that! This is for TV! There are rules, Marty! I thought he was going to say nice things."

Marty's face screwed up like he might cry. "He's in a bad mood. He was saying nice things yesterday."

Amber looked from Marty to the auditorium door. It was obvious she didn't know what to do. Apparently the rules didn't say how to handle a parrot with a filthy mouth. Looked pretty obvious to me, though—I'd go ahead and let the sucker talk. Heck, it had to be the funniest thing I'd seen all day. Anything that makes Marty Bollinger's ears turn pink is a keeper, in my book.

Beulah stubbed out her cigarette in the overflowing ashtray, walked over to Amber, and snatched the clipboard away from her. She took a pen from behind her ear and scribbled Marty's name out. "You're cut, kid. Sorry. Can't have a foul-mouthed bird on the show. FCC rules. Suzy Smith and Buttons? You're up."

Patrick let loose with another stream of expletives as Marty hustled, head down and embarrassed, toward the exit. It was too bad. That bird could've made television history.

Suzy Smith turned out to be some fifth grader and Buttons was her guinea pig. Beulah looked them over, to make sure Buttons wasn't going to cuss her out, I guess, and then sent them in. Beats me what a guinea pig was planning for a talent. I was too fixated on the door. Still no sign of them. I was going to kill Tina.

I didn't pay much attention to the next bunch of contestants. I figured it didn't matter much in the long run what they did. I even missed Trey and the fabulous bug-eating Sparky. But then Ty nudged me in the ribs.

"Arlie, check it out. Ted's up."

Donna Cavillari and Ted had shown up and were making their way into the auditorium. I figured they'd been playing by the same playbook as Mr. Boots—you know, coming late to find your center and whatnot. Or rather, they were playing by Mr. Boots's fake playbook. They both looked really composed and professional. This could not be good.

Music started up in the auditorium. "Music? They have music?"

Ty shrugged. "Most of the acts have had music. And costumes. Haven't you noticed?"

Well, no. I'd been too busy freaking out. But I wasn't about to miss Ted's audition.

I snuck over to the swinging auditorium doors and stuck my head in. I have to say, it was an impressive performance. No doubt about that. Ted was all decked out in lederhosen and embroidered suspenders, and he was definitely a pro at the yodeling. I'd expected that, though. What I hadn't expected was for him to do it while alternately walking on a barrel, eating fire, and standing on his head. And, seriously, I didn't even know dogs could do jazz hands.

I slunk back over to Ty and thunked my head against the window.

Ty patted me on the back sympathetically. "That bad, huh?"

I did my best to nod without knocking myself out. "That bad. Jazz hands, Ty."

Ty tried to whistle. I only know because of the spit that sprayed against the back of my neck. I've got to talk to him about that. "That's bad."

I plodded over to Amber, who was watching through the swinging doors and tapping her feet in time to some cat's interpretive-dance performance with yarn. "Do you have a cell phone?"

Amber nodded and handed over a flashy red number without looking at me. "No problem."

I dialed our number at home, but no one answered. I was so dead. I handed the cell phone back to Amber and plodded back to the window.

"Wish me luck, Arlie! I'm next!" Mandy had Puffkins

under one arm and her duffel bag under the other. "I'm so nervous!"

"You'll be great," I said, trying to be enthusiastic. But it was hard to work up any emotion other than dread. Because if Mandy was coming up, that meant that Mr. Boots was next.

Ty went over to the door and stood in the opening, watching the street. "You go see Mandy. I'll let you know," he said. His face was grim.

I went over to the door and watched Mandy set up. She'd arranged Puffkins as a kind of patriotic lump in an elaborate stage set, complete with bunting and flags. Along with his apparently flame-retardant stars-and-stripes getup, Puffkins was wearing some kind of headband with lots of foot-long antennas coming out of it. I wasn't sure what that was supposed to be, but I figured it would all be clear soon.

Mandy set a boom box on the edge of the stage, popped in a CD, and climbed up to Puffkins. She had just gotten to him when I heard Ty yell behind me.

"Mr. Boots!"

Mr. Boots had streaked through the open door, can o' Poppy bones still in his mouth. Tina and Deputy Hotstuff were close on his heels. That dog must have jaws of steel to carry that can that long.

Ty did his best baseball slide to grab Mr. Boots, but he totally missed. Ty's never been a strong baseball player, so I wasn't surprised. It looked good, though.

Mr. Boots dodged through feet and pets and scurried into the auditorium.

Amber grabbed me by the arm. "Arlie, stop him! He's going to mess up Mandy's performance!"

I didn't see what I could do, though. Mandy was already lighting the antennas on Puffkins's headband. Apparently, they were sparklers. When they were all lit, she did a small curtsy.

"Now, Puffkins will entertain you with a dance."

Mandy gave Puffkins an encouraging thumbs-up, hopped off the stage, and clicked the play button on the boom box. And then all hell broke loose.

CHAPTER 14

MAYBE IT'S MY FAULT. MAYBE IF I'D BEEN MORE up on my country music, I would've known we had a problem the second that song started, and I could've done something. But, instead, I was focused on trying to coax Mr. Boots and his bony pal out from under an auditorium seat.

The low moaning sound was the first sign that something was really wrong. It started almost the minute the music kicked in, and it wasn't long before it had turned into a hair-raising wail. At first I thought Mandy had just done a really crappy job dubbing the tape, but when the sound started making my skin crawl, I realized nobody does that bad a job. It had to be Cuddles.

Puffkins was sitting motionless onstage—no surprise there—but the noise seemed to have paralyzed the judges, too. Misty Morgan and Tucker Tannon had frozen fearful expressions on their faces and were clutching the arms of their seats. I'm guessing most of the auditions they saw didn't come with creepy surround sound.

I didn't blame them, though. The hair on my neck was standing up, so I left Mr. Boots to his own devices and started scanning the room for the source of the noise. Since Puffkins was just sitting onstage, head lit up like a Zen firecracker, I figured it had to be something else. Ty scooted over next to me, looking concerned. "What's up?"

I scanned the room again, but nothing seemed out of place. Then the explosions started. "Something bad, Ty. Something real bad." And Arlie wins the understatement of the year award.

The cameras set up at the side of the stage were the

first to go, in one huge dramatic flash, which would've been great on the Fourth of July but was kind of horrifying at a pet audition. Then, one by one, the lights just started randomly exploding in a shower of sparks. I ducked down next to Mr. Boots's seat. Ty scooted in next to me. Irritated that we were invading his space, Mr. Boots and his can took off for parts unknown.

"What the hell is happening?" Ty said, covering his head with a clipboard. It looked like Amber's, but I couldn't figure how he'd gotten it.

I just shook my head and watched the lights going off one by one. Then suddenly everything clicked. And believe me, once it did, I cursed the day I'd decided that Hot Country 97.5 was a lame radio station.

"Ty, listen. That song." Crazy though it might sound, the explosions weren't random.

"It's 'Elvira.' That song by the Oak Ridge Boys," Ty said, frowning. How he knew that, I'll never know. "Hey, isn't that the song that made Cuddles flip out?"

"Exactly."

Ty's eyes widened. "Oh, man. We're so screwed."

Not only did I bring Cuddles to a school full of animals that he didn't like, where his former owner was hanging out with her new pet, but I made him listen to his most hated song in the world.

Those lights were exploding in time with the lyrics. Every time the Oak Ridge Boys sang that chorus of "a oom pa-pa oom pa-pa mow mow," a different light would explode. I'm not kidding here—those were the lyrics. I couldn't make something like that up if I tried. And now, confession time. I didn't blame Cuddles for hating that song. If I had to hear that repeatedly, I might just turn into a psycho hamster vigilante too.

Ty nudged me in the ribs, listening intently. "Arlie. Did they just say 'giddyup'?" Ty asked.

I nodded. The lyrics did indeed seem to include the word "giddyup."

I stared at Puffkins, still sitting motionless on the stage with his head ablaze, and tried to figure out what to do. Cuddles was lashing out, and it was understandable.

That didn't make it any better, though. Those lights were hot, and those sparks were real. I could already see tiny singe marks on the carpet. Puffkins might be flame-retardant, but the rest of us weren't. One wrong explosion could light this place up like a torch.

I ducked as the lights overhead blew up. This was definitely not my best-case scenario come to life. I had just decided to scrap trying to make a plan and make a break for it when the chair right in front of us exploded in a huge puff of cotton and springs. I shielded my eyes. I hadn't even realized chairs were explosive.

"Arlie, the chairs!" Ty gasped.

I gritted my teeth. I'd had enough. Sure, undead angst is understandable, as is an unreasonable hatred of particularly irritating and catchy music. But when furniture starts exploding three inches from my face, all bets are off. I had to stop Cuddles. And the only way I could think to do that was to stop that damn song.

"The music, Ty! We've got to turn it off!" I grabbed Ty's clipboard to use as a shield and wove through erupting mushroom clouds that used to be auditorium seats to get to that boom box. Ty was right behind me, dodging fluffy shrapnel of his own.

I was going to stop that music if I had to whack the boom box repeatedly to do it. Truthfully, I was hoping some kind of whacking would be involved, because I was sick of taking Cuddles's crap. This was not my idea of a relaxing week without the parents.

I was halfway to the boom box when I stepped on something round that made me slip and land flat on my butt. I just avoided smacking my head against the carpet and looked up into a pair of seriously pissed off little bulgy eyes. My heart stopped for a second before I realized I recognized that face. And, thankfully, it wasn't from seeing it glowing in my closet. It was Mr. Boots. I'd stepped on Poppy's can.

I'd set the can rolling down the aisle into the orchestra pit, and after giving me the hairy eyeball, Mr. Boots took off after it. I scrambled up to go after him.

Ty hesitated, but I waved him on. "Just turn it off!"

I screamed. Getting rid of that music was the only way to stop Cuddles. As for me, I knew I'd be hearing that "a oom pa-pa oom pa-pa mow mow" in my head for years.

Mr. Boots barreled down the sloped aisle after the runaway can, and for a minute it actually looked like he was going to catch up with it. But unfortunately for him, his stopping skills aren't what they used to be. Instead of catching up with the can and retrieving it, he overtook it and slammed right into a freestanding light pole.

I was halfway down the aisle when I realized the light stand was teetering back and forth. It was going down, and Mr. Boots was right in its path.

I did my own best baseball slide, which probably looked more like a belly flop to the untrained eye. It scraped the skin off both of my elbows and seriously bruised my wrist, but it didn't matter—I grabbed Mr. Boots by the collar and jerked him out of the way just as the light pole came crashing down onto the floor. Mr. Boots was safe. But Poppy wasn't so lucky.

The light pole smashed right down onto Poppy's can of bones and erupted in a huge flash of light just as Ty managed to hit the switch on the boom box. You could actually see the electricity dancing around the pole and the can. I shivered and clutched Mr. Boots closer. He would have been completely charbroiled.

"Elvira" cut out, and was replaced by some kind of slow waltz music, I guess from the radio. Ty must've hit the wrong switch. The explosions immediately stopped, and the room flashed bright white and then went completely dark. The only light came from Puffkins onstage, who seriously must've been in some kind of trance, because I don't know how he hadn't moved the entire time.

I hugged Mr. Boots close, but I didn't move. Nobody made a sound. Aside from that waltz, the room was filled with an eerie silence, as if the whole room was holding its breath, waiting. But I didn't know what we were waiting for.

I had just decided that I was being silly, when I saw

Ty raise his arm and point at the aisle. He didn't say a word, he just pointed, trembling finger and everything. I didn't even want to look. Mr. Boots did, though, and gave a tiny strangled scream. Something down the aisle was moving. Something was coming out of Poppy's can.

If I had to swear to what I saw, I'd say it was a hamster. It was bigger than usual, and its fur had a weird glowy sheen to it, which I guess is to be expected when your can has just become Electricity Central. It looked way too small to be Cuddles, though, and the way it moved was almost dainty.

"Poppy?" I breathed. I looked over at Ty, and he nodded. He had the same idea. Undead hamster number two, come on down.

I immediately wished I hadn't thought that, because that's exactly what Poppy started to do. Without a sound, she started to drift down the aisle toward me. I have to admit, it scared the crap out of me. Cuddles was bad enough, but this little girl hamster was seriously creepy.

The last thing I wanted her to do was to come over and socialize.

She kept drifting closer. I weighed my options and decided that my best bet was to make a break for it. So call me a coward. I've been called worse. But when Poppy was about three feet away, she stopped abruptly and turned away from me, almost like she'd heard something. But as far as I could tell, there wasn't anything to hear, except that soft music.

But then I saw him. There, in the shadow under the seats, a pair of glowing eyes looked out at us.

I held my breath. I'll never doubt again. Ty was a genius.

I don't want to get mushy here, but it was the most romantic hamster reunion I've ever seen. Cuddles and Poppy drifted closer and closer to each other, and then suddenly, Cuddles came out into the open. It was the first time I'd gotten a really good look at him, and I have to admit, it's not really what I expected. Sure, he was big and all, but not a giant or anything. And he had this soft expression on his face that didn't say maniacal killer to me. I think it must've been Poppy's influence.

He reached out his little hamster arm and touched Poppy's paw. Then they drifted up onto the stage, doing a strange little dance that was almost a waltz. Seriously, with steps and everything, like they were tiny instructors at the Arthur Murray Hamster Dance School and we were their students.

It sounds weird as hell, and it really was, but they were the most graceful little hamster dancers I've ever seen. Way better than the ones on that website. They could've gone on *Dancing with the Stars* and beaten the pants off the competition.

Mr. Boots squirmed, and I clamped him tighter to my chest. There was no way I was going to distract from this moment. Mostly because it seemed like a once-in-a-lifetime kind of thing, but also because I thought if I did, Cuddles might get ticked and rip me a new one. He could do it too, I had no doubts.

The two of them did their little dance across the

stage, bathed in the light of an unblinking Puffkins, and then slowly drifted back up the aisle. They did one last final twirl outside of Poppy's can and then disappeared inside.

I stared at the can for a long second, but they didn't come back out. It was over.

The remaining lights came back on in a flash and the sparklers on Puffkins's head finally fizzled out. And Tucker and Misty leaped to their feet and burst into applause.

"That was amazing! How did you train them to do that?" Tucker ran over to Mandy, who had slumped down near the edge of the stage, and started shaking her hand violently. I thought her arm was going to come off, that's how enthused he was. Mandy looked like she was in a daze. I don't even think she realized her hand was being shaken.

Misty came over to me. "Very dramatic! Such cute moves! It's too bad about these lights, though. We must've overloaded the electrical system. We'll get that fixed right up. Congratulations, girls! You have a winner here!" She beamed at me and Mandy. Poor Mandy looked like she was going to throw up.

Puffkins took a long look around, gave an enormous sneeze, and stalked up the aisle without a backward glance. I think he'd had it with show business.

Ty hurried over, grabbed the can, and slapped the lid on tight. "Come on, Arlie. Let's get out of here."

I nodded and hurried after him up the aisle.

Misty looked perplexed. "Are you taking the little dancers? We'll need them to stay! I don't think the cameras got that."

"Yeah, sorry about that, they need to rest," I called over my shoulder as I booked it out of there. I wasn't sure what we were going to find when we opened that can, but I really didn't think Misty Morgan would want to see it.

Tina was standing at the door to the auditorium, shooting death rays at me with her eyes. "Great going, Arlie. Way to help the competition."

I gave her an apologetic smile and handed a dazed

Mr. Boots over to her. He was making some weird chatty mouth motions. I don't think the audition experience was good for him.

Amber hustled up and started rubbing Mr. Boots's ears like mad. "Oh, Mr. Boots! You're up next, but I don't know what we're going to do!" She clutched Mr. Boots's head and looked around desperately. "Wow, Puffkins really overdid it!"

"I think they said electrical problems—not Puffkins. They blew fuses," I shot back as we hurried through the entryway.

Me and Ty took off running as soon as we hit the steps, and we didn't stop until we were halfway home. Then we collapsed on a grassy patch by the side of the road. I put the can between us.

"What now?" I said.

Ty pointed at the can. "We open it."

I nodded. Opening that can was the last thing I wanted to do, but I knew the suspense would kill me if I didn't. I had to know what was inside.

I grabbed a stick and poked at the lid until it loosened. I never claimed to be brave, okay? I've seen enough horror movies to know that if you open something to see if an evil supernatural being is inside, it leaps out, suctions itself to your face, and sucks your brains out. I wasn't taking any chances.

The lid loosened and fell off. Me and Ty leaned forward to look inside.

Bones. I reached for the lid and put it back on. "I saw two skeletons. You?"

Ty nodded. "Same here."

I sighed heavily. It really was over. Cuddles and Poppy were gone.

CHAPTER 15

WHEN I GOT HOME AFTER THE AUDITIONS, MY room was completely clean—not one sign of Cuddles was left anywhere. I looked everywhere but I couldn't turn up one cardboard standee arm, hamster toy, or even a sunflower seed. Deputy Hotstuff had fixed up the kitchen door so well that you'd never have known it had been half gnawed down. He'd even replaced the curtains. It was almost like the whole thing had all been a bad dream. But any doubts I had that it was true ended the second I set foot outside my door the next day.

It was the hot news all over town how Puffkins and two mystery hamster dancers had stolen the show at the auditions. Tina would have been raging mad, but since she'd been on the scene, she was a minor celebrity in her own right. Thankfully it didn't matter in the end, anyway. The "electrical problems" in the auditorium ruined all the footage from the auditions (heck, the cameras, too), so no one made it onto the show after all.

Beulah said that they'd be back on their next round of auditions, but I had my doubts. I'd seen Tucker's and Misty's faces during the whole explosive evening. There's no way they were setting foot in this town again. Marty Bollinger was convinced the whole thing was rigged, and went around town bad-mouthing *America's Most Talented Pets* to anyone who would listen. I can't even repeat what his parrot Patrick said.

Mom and Dad were due back later that day, so me and Ty decided we'd scope out the damage to the auditorium while I still had a chance. And we would have too, if I hadn't opened my kitchen door and stepped into a real-life crime drama.

I'd heard the sirens from inside, but I hadn't really paid attention, except to make sure they weren't coming for me. They weren't. But they seemed awfully close, so I went out to do a little pre-auditorium investigating. My jaw practically hit the driveway when I saw what was going on out there. Forget the auditorium. I was just in time to see Sheriff Shifflett leading Mr. and Mrs. Knoble out to the police car in handcuffs.

Ty was sitting on the stoop, watching and eating a bag of chocolate candy. "This is awesome, Arlie. You've got a ringside seat." He popped a piece of candy into his mouth.

"What the heck?" I gaped at Mrs. Knoble. She was fighting with Shifflett every step of the way, and she had a mouth on her that would rival Patrick's. She was using every word in her secret vocabulary to describe Sheriff Shifflett, his ancestors—heck, even his pets. Not that he has any pets, but I don't think she really cared.

Mr. Knoble seemed to be more resigned. He just pulled his jacket over his head and ducked into the police car as quickly as possible. It was almost like he knew it was coming.

I plopped down next to Ty. Talk about luck. There was no way Mom was going to be mad at me and Tina for anything we had done while they were gone, since we had obviously been under extremely poor and criminal supervision. And whose fault was that? Sure not mine.

Sheriff Shifflett must've spotted me and Ty watching the sideshow, because he said something to Deputy Hotstuff and headed over to us. I couldn't help but notice that Tina was over there too, hanging on to the Deputy's ever word. I snorted. Those two had become quite an item.

"Well, well, well!" Shifflett boomed at me. I squirmed and gave a little wave. I didn't think I'd done anything to get into trouble, but heck, you never know. Shifflett didn't look upset, though—if anything, he looked pleased.

"If it isn't my little brain wave, as I live and breathe."

He stood in front of me and hooked his thumbs into his belt. I looked around. Nobody'd ever called me their little "brain wave" before, and I wanted to make extra sure he was talking about me before I opened my big mouth.

Ty elbowed me in the ribs. "Yup, there she is!"

I shot Ty a dirty look and squinted up at Shifflett. "What do you mean?"

He smiled down at me. "Giving me that idea about the Knobles, you know, helping me put their crime wave into perspective. If you hadn't pointed me in their direction, this case might've taken a lot longer to blow open." He took off his hat and wiped his forehead. "We would've solved it, mind you, but it might've taken some time."

I felt really confused. "But I didn't point you toward the Knobles!"

Sheriff Shifflett gave a barky laugh. "Sure, you did! Remember? Maybe it just looks like vandals are targeting the Knobles? Maybe that's what somebody wants you to think? Your words, missy."

I couldn't do anything but stare. "Really?"

"'Course, turns out the Feds already had a man on the case. Perkins over there—they sent him in under-cover couple a months ago. Hey, Perkins!" Shifflett yelled to a man who was talking to reporters in front of the Knobles' house. When he heard Shifflett, he looked over and gave us a wave.

Ty shot me a triumphant look. Perkins the under-cover man was the shifty eyed guy at the ice cream shop Ty had been convinced was a spy. I was never going to hear the end of this.

"So what did they do?" I was feeling super guilty. I hadn't meant to implicate the Knobles in anything—I'd just wanted to throw Shifflett off Cuddles's trail. If I could get them off the hook, I'd do it, even if it meant spending quality time at Knoble Central.

Shifflett snorted. "Hell, what didn't they do? Embezzle-ment, fraud, cooking the books—you name it. Al Knoble was in debt up to his eyeballs. He just trashed those busi-nesses to get the insurance money, and then he was planning to skip town. Would've worked too, if he hadn't gotten sloppy at that last place. Left his fingerprints all over a gas can out back. Amateur." Shifflett sniffed in disgust.

I raised my eyebrows at Ty. So maybe the Knobles really were dirty crooks. Wow, who knew?

I looked back over at the police cars just in time to see my parents' car slowly creeping up the street. They were home early, and boy were they in for a shock.

Shifflett saw the car too, and cussed under his breath. "Better go explain the situation. You girls had some shady characters watching over you. Excuse me, now." He put his hat back on and headed out to explain things to my parents. I have to admit, I was pretty glad to be off the hook for that one.

I looked around for Mr. Boots and found him pretty much where I'd expected, sprawled on his back sunning his underside in the most porny way possible. Mom was not going to be pleased about that. Welcome home, guys.

I waited nervously as my parents drove up and got out of the car. I threw one of Ty's candies at Mr. Boots to try to get him to turn over and hide his bits, but he just scowled at me and closed his eyes. Great. First the Knobles and then Mr. Boots—heck, Mom might as well get right back into the car, because she'd be needing another vacation after today.

Mom slammed the car door and came over to me. She looked all smiley and tan, so at least the resort had done some good. She patted me on the head.

"Wow, Arlie, quite a turn of events here! Sheriff Shifflett was just telling us about the Knobles. I'm so surprised! We'll get unpacked and you can tell us all about it. Hi, Tyrone," she said, smiling at Ty.

She walked up to Mr. Boots and stared down at him. He opened one eye and wagged his tail, but refused to cover up. I waited for the explosion.

Instead, Mom leaned down, picked him up, and kissed him on the head. "Hello, my little Mr. Boots! Such a cutie! Did you have a good time while we were gone? I know someone who's going to get some Snaus-ages tonight!" She put him back down and trotted inside. Mr. Boots immediately flipped onto his back for maximum perviness, but Mom didn't bat an eye.

Me and Ty gaped after her. Okay, seriously. Who was that lady and what did she do with my mother? Dad came up the walk carrying their luggage.

"Hey, kiddo," he said, and shot a significant look after my Mom. "Hypnotherapy. She thinks Mr. Boots is wearing a sarong. Doctors at the resort swear by it." He winked at us. "Don't set her straight, okay?"

I nodded.

Mr. Boots watched as Dad went inside and then grumbled to himself. He looked seriously disappointed. Talk about ruining his fun. He turned over in disgust and crawled gloomily into a discarded fuchsia tube top from his failed stripper routine. Poor guy. You know he's depressed when he dresses himself.

Ty turned to me. "So, tonight, then? I'll bring the shovels."

I nodded. "Tonight."

We'd decided that Poppy and Cuddles deserved a real grave, and luckily we just happened to know one that was empty. The plan was to go back tonight and rebury them. The plan also included large amounts of tuna, just in case Puffkins showed up and was cranky.

Ty gave me a high five and headed off down the street. I scooted over next to Mr. Boots.

I patted his back and he leaned up against my leg. The police cars were all driving away. I chucked Mr. Boots under the chin. "Wow, Mr. Boots. Big week, huh?"

Mr. Boots looked up at me. "I rove you."

I grinned at Mr. Boots and put my finger up to my lips. What Tina doesn't know won't hurt her.

THE DAILY SQUEALER

SUPERNATURAL DANCING HAMSTERS SPOTTED AGAIN!

Sources tell this reporter that the two supernatural hamster dancers that mesmerized onlookers during the auditions for the national television show TV'S MOST TALENTED PETS were spotted again late last night, this time dancing around a tree near the BURKE-MCGEE home.

When asked if she had observed this phenomenon, MANDY BURKE, a resident of the home, denied any knowledge. Her boyfriend, identified as TREY CALLAHAN, refused to comment, except to request that these photos (see below), taken at the time of our interview and showing him dressed as a disco cowboy, not be published.

(CONTINUED ON PAGE 7)

ARREST OF KNOBLE SYNDICATE REVITALIZES SHIFFLETT REELECTION CAMPAIGN

"I'll definitely vote for Buck Shifflett now!" say delighted voters. MORE—PAGE 4

OTHER ARTICLES: PAGE 6

YODELING WONDER DOG "TED" SIGNS CONTRACT TO BE SPOKESDOG FOR RICOLA COUGH DROPS

HAMSTER TANGO: HOW CAN MY RODENTS LEARN?

MR. BOOTS'S NEW SUMMER WARDROBE:
HE'S BACK AND HE'S FABULOUS

ALSO, PAGE 2:

"MY ALLERGIES ARE KILLING ME": CONFESSIONS OF A PEPPER SHAKER

NIGHT OF THE LIVING LAWN ORNAMENTS

WHO KNEW A PLASTIC PINK FLAMINGO COULD BE SO EVIL?

By Emily Ecton

When Arlie, Ty, and the ever-present Mr. Boots discover an old dragonfly pendant, they don't think much of it—it's just another thing to keep Mr. Boots from trying to swallow. But when the pendant turns out to have odd powers—powers to make all of the lawn ornaments and decorations in town come to life—it's time for Arlie and Ty (and Mr. Boots, if they can drag him out from under the couch cushions) to put a stop to all this supernatural nonsense!